THE BEAUTY QUEEN OF BONTHE

AND OTHER

STORIES OF WEST AFRICA

Gregory A. Barnes.

FriendsPress

Philadelphia

2018

Other Books by Gregory A. Barnes:

Jane among Friends (Novel)
> *What a delightful and imaginative book!   Who would have thought that Jane (wife of Lord Greystoke,) was a Quaker, who becomes close friends with an intellectually curious 400 pound gorilla. . .? Much to enjoy!*
> Lee Junker

A Centennial History of the American Friends Service Committee
Philadelphia's Arch Street Meeting House: A Biography
A Biography of Lillian and George Willoughby, 20th Century
Quaker Peace Activists
The American University: A World Guide
A Wind of Change (Novella)

ISBN-13: 978-1721926565

This book may be ordered at Quakerbooks.org, Amazon.com, or CreateSpace.com

"The Beauty Queen of Bonthe" and *Other Stories of West Africa* is dedicated in gratitude to Walter Carrington, Director, and my fellow Volunteers in Peace Corps group Sierra Leone I (1961-63):

Pat Morse Arceneaux

Alfred Arkley

Rochelle Clifton Auletta

Sandra Barnes

Elizabeth "Cindy" Juul Breen

Billie Ann Day

George Dewan

Carl Ehmann

Elizabeth Grace Ehmann

Joe Froehlich

Robert Gelardin

Bruce Gilbert

Joan Hero Hadlock

Rex Jarrell

Loren Jenkins

Roberta Rabinoff Kaplan

Dan Keil

George Lavelle

Chuck Lester

Alan MacIvor

Chuck McDowell

Ellis McKinnon

Elizabeth Roseberry

Jim Rusk

Ruthena Rusk

Sue Sadow

Will Salsberg

Gary Schulze

Clarence Sever

Jim Sheahan

Murray Stern

Tom Torrell

John Weinberg

Jamie Whitbeck

Mike Woldenberg

Ken Wylie

Staff: Mike McCone, Deputy Director; Jane Campbell Beaven, training officer; and Bill Elsea and Paul Guise, Physicians

Table of Contents

Acknowledgments

I have dedicated this book to my fellow members of Peace Corps group Sierra Leone I—many now alas departed—and add here my thanks for their enduring friendship. I have a special appreciation for one of them in particular: Gary Schulze, who provided photos that inspired the cover design, and who has been in effect our group's ongoing ambassador to Sierra Leone. In 2014, Gary became an "Officer of the Order of The Rokel," Sierra Leone's highest civilian award; he has also been named an Honorary Paramount Chief in Sierra Leone, for his ongoing contact and contributions to the country spanning more than half a century.

I am indebted to many others for help over the years on these stories, more than I can name. Those who assisted me recently in shaping the 4 of the 7 stories that have not been previously published are Fatima Iya, Grace Gonglewski, and Ed Jakmauh, each of them with specialized knowledge. Long years ago, Sandra Theis Barnes provided support and the necessary tough criticism of many of these works in their embryonic form. In later years, Yoko Koike Barnes provided constant encouragement and wisdom as I sought out the truth in my various efforts and got ready to let them fly.

I also thank my Quaker community in Central Philadelphia Monthly Meeting for supporting me in my authorship, and appreciate Quakerbooks for carrying my work Finally, I want to offer my respects to the boys I taught at Jimmi Bagbo Secondary School and my hope that they have had long and fulfilling lives.

Introduction

President John F. Kennedy electrified American idealists in 1961 with his creation of the Peace Corps. Legions of young and old saw a chance to serve their country and underdeveloped lands in nonviolent ways, and my then-wife, Sandra Theis Barnes, and I responded to the call. We served first as Volunteers in Sierra Leone (1961-63) and thereafter in the then-Northern Region of Nigeria, where I acted as Associate Director (1963-65).

The works in this volume were created during this period, when I was learning to be a writer. I published several stories while they were fresh off my old Olympia typewriter, one of which is included here—as well as my novella, *A Wind of Change,* which is not included.

The other stories in this volume needed time to mature while I learned more about making them true. Two of the stories reprinted here have been published in the 21st century. All but the first have undergone scrutiny at various points in the half-century since I experienced the hospitality of various West African peoples and the extraordinary changes under way at that time: the ending of British colonial rule, the transition of long-colonized people into leadership roles, and the new tensions engendered both by the interaction of the many ethnic groups living even in the smallest of these countries and by the conflicting roles of traditional leaders, colonial officers, missionaries, aid workers and the new men (they were almost all men) under the recently established governments. The 1960's in that region of the world strikes me as an epically dynamic scene of cultural change.

The events described in these 7 stories may be largely imagined but the conflicts depicted are true to life. The most impressionistic of the collection evokes the mystery of the world I encountered in my experience as a Volunteer teaching in a remote village. I offer up an event that still mystifies me: a student fractured his arm late in the fall semester; as driver of one of only two automobiles in our village, I rushed him to the hospital in Bo, 35 miles away, where he submitted to X-rays but refused surgery or even a cast, choosing instead to consult a native healer back in our village; I saw him a day later with (apparently) mud all over his arm, which was encased in a sling so tight that it made his skin bubble out here and there; yet only a couple of weeks later, he wrote (with that arm) his final exams. My story, "A Day along the Tonkolili Road" relates similar "impossible" events that add to the West African mystique; Tonkolili exists only as a nice African-like sound for an enchanted place. Why I should celebrate my own naivety is perhaps odd; I believe my acceptance of my own ignorance improved in the writing of the story; in a sense I was laughing at my own confusion.

Elsewhere, even place names and other identifiers remain intact except where discretion forbids. The incidents that generated the stories are those I may have witnessed only fleetingly or glancingly: So, I pass by a police station one evening in Kano, the great Nigerian entrepot, when it is strangely lit up, and a Peace Corps Volunteer I am visiting explains that beggars are being rounded up and bused out of town. On a trip to Senegal I encounter a remarkable concrete staircase that rises up over the breakers and rocks of the sea, for a purpose I cannot imagine. In the village where I teach as a volunteer, I am summoned with my primitive first-aid kit and no medical training to the side of a young diamond miner dying of pneumonia.

Most memorably, I deliver a new volunteer to an assignment in central Nigeria where, as I discover, he will displace an English colonial servant. The Englishman is just discovering the dismissal himself. He turns his face but not his body toward me when we meet. I have no recollection of what he said but the look he gives me lingers in my memory; I even remember his name all these decades later. Finally, while visiting Peace Corps chums on Sherbro Island, I heard about an Irish priest who seemed to expect too much understanding of Catholic mysticism from a young Sierra Leonean woman, who was probably not, I confess, a beauty queen.

Now in age I have wondered how well my stories reflect the SPICES that govern my behavior as a Quaker—that is, Friends' concerns for Simplicity, Pacifism, Integrity, Community, Equality, and Stewardship. I like to believe that in these stories I already demonstrate a belief in that of God in everyone.

FAITH, HOPE, LOVE

(Reprinted from *The Grecourt Review* [Smith College] viii, 2 [April 1965], 9-18)

They watched the approaching rain, the three of them: Foday, in his robes; Pastor Flint in his customary white short-sleeve shirt and pants; an Mrs. Flint, in a thin, worn dress. Next to their visitor the Flints were both very white, perhaps from advancing years. The Pastor was above sixty, and mindful enough of his deteriorating health to talk (though not very seriously) of going home to retire.

Conversation had fallen off, as happens in Africa, where no one feels the need to sustain it. The three of them looked quietly at the blackening skies they knew so well. In ten minutes, Foday would have to leave; he would have another ten minutes to get to his home in the village before the rains fell. He stirred slightly. He was a man of no little physical beauty, with a strong, handsome head and a sinewy physique marred only by a mangled right hand, which he kept under his robe. His manner of speaking was casual, yet contained something regal.

"It is very kind of you to give me more pills.". He held up, in his left hand, a small white container.

"It's quite all right, Foday."

"My wife will be very grateful," he said. He expressed his gratitude more strongly than he would to any one else. Europeans—at least, Mrs. Flint—seemed to expect it.

"Take her our love," said the Pastor. "And tell her we hope she'll be well again soon."

"Why do you suppose your family has so much trouble with fever?" said Mrs. Flint.

"I would like to know, too," said Foday. "Always, someone has fever, and I must somehow find medicine.'

"We understand," said the Pastor.

"If you did not help me, I think some of my family would die."

"Why, we're glad to help you, however we can," said the Pastor, and Mrs. Flint too smiled. This was something all the people noticed, that Pastor and Mrs. Flint were most happy when they thought they were helping someone.

The cook was now stirring about the kitchen, preparing the Flints' supper (and so much food there would be!); since, too, the air had become abruptly still, and the rain was imminent, Foday stood to leave.

"I have seen you," he said, gathering his robe together.

"Thank you for coming" said the Pastor. "We're always glad to have you."

"Yes, thank you" said his wife.

Foday nodded, and sauntered away. He stood as straight as the staff he used to support him, and carried his head in such a way that his eyes might look directly toward heaven. Judged from his bearing alone he was a proud man, too proud in fact to expose the bad right hand.

"Lee, Lee," said the Pastor's wife, as they watched him go, "won't you ever draw the line with that boy?"

"Now, Dear," the Pastor replied, "Foday can't afford medicine these days. We have to give him a helping hand."

"But all the pills he asks for! You'd think he was setting up a hospital. You know he was never this unhealthy as a boy, and I don't remember Adama being sickly when he first married her. I think he's taking care of all his brothers and sisters too, and their children."

'Well—well, that's all right. It means we're helping more people."

"We can't help everybody."

"But Foday's a special case, Mildred," said the Pastor. "He's a good boy, always has been. I'd do the same for any good friend who'd fallen on hard times."

His wife nodded wearily. "I know, but you gave him all but the last four quinine tablets. I don't think I'd mind except for that."

"We'll be going to town in a week or so anyway. I'll get more pills then."

"How many? Four or five bottles, so you'll have enough for Foday?"

The Pastor chuckled.

"Well, do as you want" she said. "Foday's a likeable boy well enough. But I must say, he's taking advantage of you."

The Pastor sighed phlegmatically; there was a fresh damp breeze blowing, and his favorite stew was simmering in the kitchen. His home was comfortable only by African standards, but it was furnished just as he and his wife might have furnished it in their own home town, and after all, it *was* home had been for thirty-one years, off and on. He lay his balding and somewhat blemished head back on the soft old chair. "Remember," he said, "remember what nice things Foday used to do for us before he lost his hand."

"I do," said Mrs. Flint. "He and Adama were both generous. Of course, it was no more than Joseph Brima or some of the others have done."

He frowned. "Maybe not. But again, maybe it was. It seems like he was always sending up a pineapple, or a couple of eggs, or a whole basket of grapefruit. Yes, I believe he was more consistent than the others."

She didn't bother to argue. Supper was ready.

Foday was little past thirty, but his manner, even from the time he had entered the men's society, was that of a village elder. He used a long and smooth walking stick which he had selected and shaped himself years before, and strode in a heavy, meditative manner. These first desultory rain drops against his lavender robe could not hurry him; he was lost in thought.

It was true he had once done the Missionary couple hundreds of small favors; eggs, oranges mangoes, yams, coffee, so many things he had sent the Pastor, and the woman had prepared African dishes for them.   But of course he owed them everything.   They had been in the village since before he could remember, and who but the Pastor had taught him to read and write, persuaded his relatives to pay his school fees, given him a meal now and then (and how he Europeans ate!), had even taken him into his home for a year; had given him money as a boy, loaned it to him as a man, and found him a job that should have ended his money problems.

Yet, after all this, he was cheating the Pastor. It was very strange how such things came to be. Three years ago he could not have imagined it, but then he had a lorry and lots of money, then he could go to great lengths to do favors for the Pastor.   There was never a need for his friend to drive his car in those days; wherever he wanted to go, Foday would take him. And he could afford to buy small gifts for the Flints, although he did so sparingly, since, being Europeans, they might soon think it necessary to give something in return. But he could have given many gifts, and he did do a number of small favors.   Those were prosperous days. If a man knew his lorry, and the roads, and could drive a bargain on fares, he might get rich hauling people and goods around the country. The farther he went each day and the faster he went, the more he earned, and Foday had learned how to make good time. In the end, this was his undoing. He sideswiped another lorry, went over an embankment and into a tree and onto his side. The truck's falling over cost him the four fingers of his right hand, with which he'd held onto the window ledge. Fortunately, no one else was in the lorry. But fortune was otherwise cold, for he had no insurance, no way to drive another lorry, no way even to use the writing ability so laboriously acquired under the Pastor's guidance. With his money gone, he had to resort to work on a brother's small farm. This kept him very poor indeed. Then the Pastor, out of kindness or pity, had offered him pills for an attack of fever, and—typically—gave him more than he needed. His people had great faith in the Missionary's medicine. He had sold six for a shilling each.

Since that first time, fourteen months ago, he had not taken a pill himself, even when he was quite ill; the woman had never seen the pills, although she knew people came to her husband for medicine. All who had fever called on him. If they couldn't pay a shilling for their pill, they brought him a small chicken or a can of rice. He didn't get enough to live on from this trade, but taken with what food he got from his brother he and his family had at least enough to eat.

Fortunately, the Pastor had heard nothing of his sales. At first Foday was nervous in the Pastor's presence, but after a time he carried on his business as a matter of course. The only effect of his visits on him was a nagging moroseness; this time it weighed heavily on his handsome shoulders. He hid the pills in the fingerless hand under the robe. When he reached his hut, just ahead of the rain, he was frowning and he grew increasingly sullen during the evening. The woman noted it, and did not speak.

The next morning he was still brooding. But he walked to his maternal home just before noon and as luck would have it there were in that village three people sick with fever and one man gave him a plump hen for two pills and another gave him a bottle full of rice for two, and a third paid a shilling for one. Food for three days and a shilling besides! The frown left his face. Half-way home he stopped, dropped the bottle and the trussed-up chicken and counted the pills left in the container. Eleven; the Pastor was very generous. Well, he no doubt had plenty for himself.

The woman had found some peppers, so that night they had chicken-and-rice that made his stomach burn happily. Later in the evening he sold three pills, for more rice, a quart of palm oil, and another shilling. He looked pleased. When, after the children were asleep, he called the woman to his bed he did not appear a man troubled by the reproofs of conscience.

In six days time he had sold all the pills. That was perhaps too fast. Now he would have to turn people away for several weeks, until it would be safe to ask the Pastor for more. And what if he should get fever himself and have no way to cure it, or someone were to go to the Pastor for pills and say that Foday Kawa usually sold pills but his were finished? He spent the next two days working for his brother, avoiding every one.

When he came in from the second day in the fields, he heard that the Pastor was sick. Gossip had a way of losing all truth among the people, but he inquired closely and extensively enough to learn that the old Missionary did have fever. That was strange; the Pastor watched his health very closely. Foday looked concerned, but—perhaps because he had no pills to offer—he didn't call at the Flint home.

About midnight Mrs. Flint roused him from his sleep. She seemed scarcely able to control herself. "Foday" she said "Pastor Flint is terribly ill. Would you please let me have all your pills?"

His left hand shot to his head, as if to control the eyes that widened unnaturally. "Missus," he said, "those pills are finished."

She looked frightened and this scared him the more, for Europeans were not like this, they feared nothing, not even devils or witches. But this weak old woman was acting just like a scared African woman, and it was a terrible thing to see. "Finished?" she repeated. "They can't be. How could you use a bottle of pills in a week? There must be some left."

"No, Missus," he said. "There's none."

For a moment she seemed about to faint. She couldn't speak, and had difficulty in keeping herself upright.

"It was my uncle," he said. "He made me give him ten."

"Oh Foday," she said, "what have you done to us?" She said a prayer to herself before his terrified eyes. Before he could speak, she hurried out and drove away, in the very old car she and the Pastor kept. He watched from his verandah. She was on her way to the town, twenty miles over rain-softened roads the helpless old woman would have to drive. She was a poor driver, and alone at this late hour. He had never known her to drive so far alone, at least under such conditions. Pastor Flint must be very sick.

Abruptly he placed his head against the wall of his hut and moaned. For several minutes he seemed immobilized. As suddenly, he went in the house, put on his sandals and robes and ran out. The walking stick, the solemn gait were forgotten; the hand was not tucked in the robe. He ran out the road to the edge of the village, where sat the Pastor's gleaming white house, atop a hill. Not until he was on the vine-covered porch did he stop; he was panting violently. He could see a light, but there was no sound. The door was open. After catching his breath, he entered, and went to the Pastor's room.

There the old man lay, alone and delirious, his face bubbling with perspiration. Foday knelt beside the bed. This was fever, very bad fever; he had seen men that looked better than the Pastor die. There was no one to treat him at this moment, when he was worst, and Mrs. Flint wouldn't be back for an hour. Foday moaned again. He was unable to look at the Pastor. Pressing his good hand against his head, he rose and retreated to the darkness of the porch. He sat there, unmoving but awake, talking to himself. "Pastor, I have failed you," he sobbed. "You were like my father, and I have killed you. God punish me for being an unworthy son. Let me die, I am unworthy. Our Father, which art in heaven," and so he continued, in a chant which relied less on words than rhythm and fervor.

Afterwards he sat quietly, his head on his hands. A small breeze brought fresh rain. It was light and lambent on his neck, but twenty miles away it might have turned the roads to paste, for rains varied greatly from town to town. Surely Mrs. Flint had found help; the Europeans always looked out for one another, and the doctors would want to help the Pastor, the good, kind old man. Everyone loved him. Where would the people of this town be without him? What would Foday's life have been without him?

In the distance he heard a motor, and he lifted his head, revealing the tears in his eyes. He watched the headlights as they swung around the hills below and dashed in and out of the trees, and then stabbed the driveway in fury. It was she, and he sucked his breath joyfully. But he did not let her see him. Before the headlights uncovered the porch, he had moved into the shadows.

Mrs. Flint was crying softly. With her was the doctor, a round little man who hurried her into the house. Foday was alone.

He endured it only a few minutes. He slipped into the house and entered the Pastor's room so quietly that the others did not notice his presence, and there he stood, watching the doctor's every move, his face lined with terror. He nor any of his friends had ever seen a European so near death. It was something he never expected to see, just as was the fear that still hung on Mrs. Flint's face. He touched her arm.

"I am here," he said.

Mrs. Flint wept harder; not the way his woman would weep, but as if she would rather burst than emit any sound.

"I am praying for my friend, the Pastor," he said.

"You," she sobbed, "because of you he may die."

He looked to the doctor, but the doctor seemed worried, and said nothing. Mrs. Flint turned away. He was again alone, for he was not welcome. As he left the house he held his head high, but once outside he let it sink, and his pace was no more stately than that of a decrepit animal. He didn't cry, but he moaned, "Aah," again, "Aah," and again. By his bed, he said a prayer: "Oh God, save our reverend Pastor. He brought me from the bonds of ignorance into Thy Saving Grace. He clothed me when I was sick. He fed me when I was hungry. He gave me drink when I was having thirst. But I was unworthy, Lord. The Devil, he tempted me, and I was not strong enough to say, 'Get thee behind me, Satan.' Save the Pastor, oh Lord, but do not spare me, for I am deserving no mercy. I can die. In Christ's name, amen."

After he crawled under the netting he lay awake until dawn and said many more prayers. He asked God to let him die.

The malaria attack left the Pastor in a feeble state for weeks, and long before he regained his health and went back to his normal routine of teaching and preaching the word got around that Foday Kawa had contracted some mysterious ailment. He ate little, slept little, spoke little and worked not at all. He couldn't or wouldn't smile; and though he looked healthy enough, he never moved from his hammock on the verandah except to go to bed. He seemed to stare through people who spoke to him without hearing them. After a week, his brother offered to pay for a trip to the doctor, but he refused. His brother waited patiently for him to come back to work on the farm, and sent food for the family, but he grew angry after a month had passed and Foday was as inert as ever; he cut his food donation to one cup of rice a day. Still Foday lolled in his hammock.

As soon as the Pastor was able, he walked down into the village to Foday's home. At first sight of the Pastor, Foday started more abruptly than he had in weeks, but he greeted the older man with some semblance of his former dignity. The Pastor was perhaps the more embarrassed of the two.

"I'm very sorry you're ill," he said.

Foday thanked him with a nod. "Perhaps I shall be well soon."

"What's wrong? Do you know?"

"No."

"I was afraid it had something to do with my own illness. Mrs. Flint told me how badly you felt."

"No, it's not that. But I'm glad you're well."

The Pastor frowned. "You mustn't feel badly about anything she may have said. She was very much upset, and didn't mean to—"

"No, no. Of course that doesn't bother me."

"Then what is it? I don't think it's fever. If you know what it is, I'll find some pills or medicine for it."

"No," Foday blurted, "I don't need pills." The Pastor's kindness was unlimited. Obviously, he bore no grudge, the way some Europeans might; if asked, he would probably give another bottle of quinine pills without a moment's hesitation.

"Well," said the Pastor, "I'll be glad to help you in any way possible."

"Thank you," said Foday. "I shall be well soon."

The Pastor smiled fondly and patted his arm before leaving.

But Foday didn't get well. Perhaps it was the Pastor's offer of pills that made him brood all the more. The Pastor liked to help people, which was why the people loved him, but his kindness to Foday was almost beyond belief. He called again and again, offering to take him to the doctor, or to buy him medicine, bringing him food and giving his children odds and ends of clothing. Foday still seemed to seek death; his friend's kindness made him, if anything, more morose.

The family began to grow sickly. The children's stomachs bulged, and the woman was weak and surly. She asked him to go back to his brother's farm, and when he demurred she demanded it, in a loud voice. Perhaps she would have left him except for the fact that the Pastor had been kind to her, too, and she knew the Pastor wouldn't approve. And every time they got so hungry they couldn't talk, there the old missionary would be, with fruit and a little rice.

During one of his visits the Pastor was breathing heavily, as a result of having walked too quickly, and it became obvious that he was aging very rapidly. Foday watched him far more attentively than he had observed anything else in the preceding weeks. Who would care for this man in his final days—assuming he didn't go home? Unfortunately, it couldn't be Foday Kawa.

But as he watched the Pastor walk slowly away, Foday started, struck by an idea. He threw his head back in contemplation; then his eyes fell on the walking stick in the corner, so long kept in readiness but unused. That was a fine staff. He had had it for years, and he had smoothed it down so perfectly that many of his friends had coveted it. The Pastor himself had said it was worthy of a chief.

He moved with resolution. First he examined the stick; his eyes lighted with pleasure to see the harmony of the colors, the swing and swirl of the grain. Then, from an old chest, he pulled his carving knife, hammer, chisel, and a pencil. He had learned carving at his father's side as a boy, to an acceptable degree of craftsmanship. How well he could do with only a thumb and palm was a question he naturally pondered, but he wasn't deterred. He was happy; he sang a little to himself. He mulled over his approach for a day, eager but careful, turning the stick this way and that. It took another day to lay out the letters with pencil around the head of the stick. "Faith, Hope, Love," he spelled, one under the other. He laughed in joyful recognition of this craftsmanship.

He set to work with his tools. It was very slow, painfully slow. He had to use his left hand a great deal. A week went by. The Pastor came to visit, and he hid the stick. He seemed in better spirits, the Pastor told him, with a pleased expression. He *was* in better spirits; he worked from morning till night on his carving, and could scarcely restrain his pleasure.

It was finished. The letters were almost perfect. His critical inspection brought "ahs" to his lips, and for two days he could scarcely look at anything else. Then, with patience and a persistent smile of satisfaction, he waited for the Pastor.

Within a week, the thoughtful old man appeared, bearing his usual load of foodstuffs. Foday put on a fresh robe to meet him. Pride suffused his face as he received the Pastor's gifts and gave them to the woman.

"Now," he said, "I have a very special gift for you." He pulled the stick from a corner—not hastily—and held it across his chest for the Pastor to receive, as a general might present his sword.

The Pastor was astonished. "Why, this is your own walking stick,' he said.

"No longer. I want you to have it, to help you when you walk. And look!" He pointed to the words he had carved.

"'Faith, Hope, Love.' Why Foday—"

"Sir?"

"Why Foday, did you do this?"

"I did." The former grandeur of Foday's bearing and manner had returned.

"Why Foday," and the old man was weeping, not much, only as his wife wept, softly and unwillingly. "With your hand--?"

Foday hid his hand. "I hope you like the stick," he said.

The Pastor could hide his eyes but not his voice. "It's the finest gift any one has ever given me," he whispered, hoarsely.

"I am very glad," said Foday. He beamed as the Pastor fondled the staff and set it to the floor with the gentleness of a caress.

The Pastor wiped his eyes and tried to pretend he hadn't wept at all. Still he could scarcely speak. He tested the stick with a few short paces and said, "It's a very fine staff."

It was not a time for words. The Pastor seemed not just touched but overwhelmed, and very embarrassed about it. It was strange that this man, who had given so much, should not know how to receive. He continued to fondle and examine the stick, staying a longer time than he usually permitted himself. At length he said a weak "good-bye" and left. Foday stared happily after him until he started up the hill to his home.

The next day Foday put on his robes and the felt cap he saved for special occasions, in preparation for a visit to the Flints. The woman, who was always sullen these days, looked at him suspiciously and said he must go to his brother's farm. He didn't argue; he said, gently, "Tomorrow I will go to the farm."

He spent the afternoon walking about the village, greeting his friends and discussing his old sickness. He had recovered, he assured them. Certainly his bearing was as regal as ever: Head high, shoulders thrown back, the gait majestic. Before the end of the day he found a new walking stick. He rejected several that he noticed on his tour, but this one, while not as fine as the last, could be smoothed into a worthy staff.

At six 'clock, when, he knew, the Flints were finished with their day's work and would be relaxing in their small front room, he made his trek up the hill. The waning sun lent a glow to his lavender robes and a gloss to his muscular black arms. As usual, the left hand held the walking stick while the right was tucked beneath the robe.

When the Pastor opened the door, he said, "I have come."

"Foday! Come in, come in," said the older man. "I want to tell you how much I'm enjoying that walking stick. It's just wonderful."

Mrs. Flint came to him. She was smiling, but she seemed embarrassed. It was the first time they'd met since she made the long trip to town. "I'm very happy to see you," she said, earnestly. "I'm sorry you were sick."

"I've recovered."

"Good," said the Pastor. "Sit down."

"It was kind of you to give the Pastor your stick," said Mrs. Flint, as they seated themselves. "I know you must have hated to part with it."

"Not at all. I was glad to give it to my friend.'

The Pastor smiled. But Mrs. Flint was troubled, and nothing was going to stop her from what she had to say. 'I hope you haven't stayed away because of what I said that night—?"

"No," said Foday. "You were quite right. It was shameful that I should not have pills for my friend."

"Well," said the Pastor, "what Mrs. Flint said probably didn't make you feel any better, but I can assure you she didn't mean to be cruel."

"She was not cruel at all."

"It was my own fault for giving away too many. I won't let that happen again, believe me. Now I have plenty of pills, for both of us.'

"Yes, Foday," said Mrs. Flint, "you'd better take some more in case you get sick again."

"No, no," he said. "I didn't have fever."

"But you might get fever," she insisted, "and what about your family?"

"Just a minute," said the Pastor; he hobbled to the back of the house and returned with three large containers of quinine tablets. "Look at these," he said. "I got a bottle especially for you.'

"But you must keep them," said Foday. "I do not want to fail you again."

"You mustn't blame yourself for that night," said Mrs. Flint. "I would have had to get a doctor anyway. And that's the truth."

The cook was setting the Flints' dinner table. Foday gave him greeting and talked with him a minute before turning again to the Missionary couple. "Adama sends her respects," he said.

"How is Adama?" asked Mrs. Flint, intensely. "It seems as though I never get down to see her any more."

And so they talked of everything but pills; of Adama and the children; of his return to his brother's farm; and of his days as a lorry driver, from which point the Pastor began to reminisce over his first years in Africa. The cook brought on the food about 6:30 and it was time for him to leave. How the Europeans ate! Always three meals a day and each meal included a meat serving. The Pastor was not a rich man, yet he had enough, it seemed.

"I have seen you,' he said, standing.

"Won't you have dinner with us?" asked Mrs. Flint.

"Yes, we really would like that," said the Pastor.

"No," he said. "Adama will be waiting."

"I'm sorry," said Mrs. Flint. "But wait—at least you must take some quinine pills. I insist on that."

"But I am well," he replied.

"Now you've had all sorts of sickness,' said the Pastor, "and you're bound to have more." He held out a container.

Foday shook his head, but Mrs. Flint took the pills and pressed them in his hand. "Please," she said. "It will make me so happy if you take them."

The frail, wrinkled woman—she too showed alarming signs of age—was pleading with him, and the Pastor's eyes showed the earnestness of his offer. The cook had laid a heaping bowl of rice on the tale and was at this moment drawing out the chairs in signal to the couple that supper was served. There was no time to argue.

"Very well," he said, "but only for my family.' He took the container and placed it in the fingerless right hand, which he immediately tucked under his robe.

A DAY ALONG THE TONKOLILI ROAD

On this cheerful Sunday morning I am seated with a second cup of coffee in my bungalow just one-half mile from Tonkolili. While I inspect a gecko crawling up my parlor wall and listen to the weaver birds and some one's goat outside, my steward clears away my breakfast crumbs. I see I'm in his way and move, to a lumpy-cushioned deck-chair by the window at the front. From here I watch the commerce on the road: the market women toting baskets on their heads; the farmers headed toward their plots; two roaring straining lorries; and my colleague Mr. Briwa, who approaches from the town.

Everyone is wearing warm attire, because the day has started cool, but this is March and soon the sun will stand above the world—just above—to drop its heat with force. Because of this, so Briwa said, Goboi will dance at 8:00. And so I rise.

He comes to my verandah in a shy uncertain step and I say *Buwa!* jocosely as I meet him at the door. He's shorter and more generously girthed than I. One notices especially his mouth, its shape a gliding hawk as seen head-on. And when he smiles—he does so now—a panoply of gold and silver fillings catches fire. He handles me with deference, in part because he hasn't solved the West, but there is also my degree—a talisman, he thinks. It's probable he doesn't know that he is much the older of us two. If he did, he might not show such ready diffidence.

—Well, I have come, he says. Politely he declines a cup of coffee, saying we are waited for in town.

I call instructions to my steward, shut my door, and take the road for Tonkolili.

Ahead of us the hill is lined with zinc-roofed homes; most are smaller than my own but one, the pink house of Oduram, the Assistant District Officer, gives evidence of far more luxury. Before the house, the red and purple bougainvillea tremble in the breeze. All colors—pink and red and violet, the thick green shrubs behind the house— are rich as local tie-dyes in the fleeting morning light. Later, when the trucks have stirred the dust and the sun revealed its spite, each striking hue will gradually turn brown.

We crest the hill and pass a man emitting bull-like roars. It is the crier, Mr. Briwa tells me, shouting that Goboi is set to dance; this will be a special fête, I see, and I am grateful, for it's been arranged especially for me.

But looking down the sloping road to town we hear more doleful sounds. I look askance at Mr. Briwa.

—There's been a death, he tells me. A local boy, at school a hundred miles away, has died. His mother just received the news; he was her last surviving son.

We soon arrive upon the somber scene, which to the unaccustomed ear sounds shockingly *pro forma*. On mats beside the road two women and a crowd of children beat the earth and wail. I'm conscious I've been hearing their lament since early on.

Mr. Briwa knows them; he wants to say a word.

—Of course, I say, and stand by ill at ease. He gives the mother solace as I take a look around. Atop the gable of the mother's house are mounted dancers cut crudely from the zinc—a piquant note. There's a field behind the house, in which a thatched shed stands; here the Limba tappers sell their palm wine. How often have I heard befuddled laughter floating from this make-shift bar. It's silent now, so early in the morning. In the distance back of it I see a rising smoke-tornado from a new farm's burning brush.

The wailing hasn't ceased. The farmers walking by, the market women, take no notice of the cries. Neither does the girl who's pounding rice behind a neighbor's house, her matchless torso gleaming from the lifting and the driving of her pestle. Now, should it bother me?

The mother gives my friend the letter, and he lets me read it with him. Purportedly it's from a relative, who claims the youngster met his end a week ago and recommends the mother come at once; but, says Mr. Briwa, the boy's his former student, and he knows the writing is that student's own!

—Why should the uncle urge the mother come? he says.

I cannot give an answer.

He says he's sure the boy himself has sent this startling letter.   He tells her this; she hushes all the mourners. The minutes pass as they talk somberly, while I, aware of time, stand wishing we were gone. At last it is resolved.

--She'll take a lorry north, friend Briwa tells me. Apologizing for the halt, he adds that we must hurry on; Goboi will not wait long. And so we leave. But on our route are passersby I know, to whom I wish to speak. One of these is Sao, who steps from her verandah as we near. She wears a close-wrapped yellow cloth that demonstrates that even though her hips, to local tastes, are slim, her *derrière*—as I have noted many times—is *comme il faut*. Prettier women live in Tonkolili but she attracts me most of all, by showing me a pertness that the others mostly lack.

"*How da body,* Sao?" I ask, and she addresses me by name; she brashly takes my hand. All the world knows she's the lover of the A.D.O., or all except his wife, they say. Mr. Briwa no doubt thinks her brazen but I release her hand reluctantly and approve once more her other side before we slip away. We pass the thatch-roof court *barrie*, then two or three small shops, and last the open market. The locus of the fête, our destination, is the town chief's private compound. We arrive, and we are seated in his *barrie*'s pleasant shade.

The performance has begun: in separate groups the men and women dodge around surrounding houses, chanting, clapping hands. Six or seven women fiercely shake their *shegburé*, the gourds ensnared by beaded strings, in syncopated cadence. Among the men are drummers and a blower of the *bufé*, the horn created from a tusk; somehow they beat and blow despite their furtive darting. One ensemble passes out of sight, the other reappears, the first emerges from a new approach.

At last a clamor starts; the instruments are synchronized; the groups come out together with Sir Goboi at their head. A splendid devil, he's said to be the Chief's own entertainer, like a monarch's private jester. His mask's a hide cap lined with mirrors and bright red strips of cloth. He's decked from shoulders down with raffia; it rustles as he paws the earth. In front he wears a deerskin (Mr. Briwa lets me know), profusely dyed, recalling knights-errants' shields. He shakes his shoulders; he makes a startling clatter that derives from wooden stakes tied in clusters on his back. On the stakes are suras from the Quran, which protect Goboi from evil.

Behind Goboi a sturdy man in shorts deploys a brush-like paddle on the devil's back, to keep him in his bailiwick. I notice young boys too, in colored paper caps, who steer Goboi away from rocks, the *barrie* and the crowd. The dust erupts and hovers.

The movements of Goboi's feet are quick and intricate but I'm attracted to the beater of the *kélé*, the hollow bamboo drum, who changes rhythm in an instant, as the devil's feet demand. The stout interpreter intrigues me too; he crawls through Goboi's legs, jumps atop his back, and flagellates him with the paddle. And all the time the women sing their riddles, clap their hands, and shake their *shegburé*. Suddenly Goboi attempts to grab a woman's head-tie, and so she takes it off.

"They may not wear their head-ties 'round Goboi," my colleague tells me. "Nor may they cross his path. They're to sing and clap their hands and that is all." Goboi advances on the *barrie* wall and capers splendidly. I offer him a coin or two, as he expects of me; Mr. Briwa adds his own. The wizardly interpreter receives the *dash* and hands it to a friend, but fast: he can't neglect his beating and his steering.

But now Goboi retreats into a hut. Can the end have come so soon? The music doesn't stop. Above the clamor Briwa tells me that the Goboi mask is heavy— *Goboi*'s the *Mendé* word for "bent" and the mask in fact will not permit the dancer's standing straight.

The singing, and the drumming, and the clapping never cease. The *kélé* drummer close to me has sweated through his ragged undershirt. The women in their light bright clothes are colorful, much more so than the men. One lady starts a pleasant ruckus: it's her complaint the men won't join the chants.

Goboi emerges from his hut. The noise crescendos as he skims across the dirt in burlap socks. Although I give him frequent tips, no new step shows itself to my unpracticed eye. But Briwa, quite the connoisseur, is more appreciative. Suddenly he grips our table: Goboi has tripped across a rock embedded in the soil. Gasps and shrieks resound around us as his interpreter reacts—too late: Goboi is on the ground.

I'm surprised to hear my friend exclaim and jump up in alarm. The music stops; at least I cannot hear it in the clamor and the swarm of startled villagers, nor can I see the drummers. Five men accost the devil's aide with streams of heated words. The women raise a fuss among themselves. Mr. Briwa shouts above the roar that this interpreter has failed a solemn duty; his customary placid face is so contorted that he seems a different man.

When I resume my focus on the whirling storm about us, I see the felled Goboi, who rises to his knees, then with assistance to his feet. He slips into the nearby hut. By now the shamed interpreter is hemmed in on all sides. Mr. Briwa moves to aid the man, as does the Tonkolili chief: they prevail upon the throng to turn him loose. The essence of their argument appears to be that rioting is scandalous before their honored guest. I am of course chagrined but glad to see the fearful miscreant released without a fight. A general debate ensues, which Briwa helpfully explains:

—The interpreter's supposed to see that Goboi does not fall. He must be punished for his negligence.

In all good time, the brisk palaver is resolved: the interpreter must be brought to court this very afternoon. Though the *melée* hasn't ceased, the excitement drops away. Mr. Briwa is excessively depressed. For him the ceremony has been ruined: he's oppressed I have not seen a *prima* Goboi dance.

I assure him I'm content but he's not mollified; indeed he launches into—seemingly—hyperbole to show me how unworthy this performer is compared to Gobois he has known. His long and curling mouth is set and grim. He now insists on walking me a way toward home, and as we leave the scene of his disgrace—for he has staged the show—he tries to meet my inquiries.

—Yes, you may watch the case this afternoon—just as you wish. No, no one will object. But it's a shameful matter nonetheless.

In front of Sao's house he leaves me, with a handshake and a woeful smile that covers up his gold and silver teeth. Other people view the case with higher spirits. Along the road they cluster, gossiping intensively, no doubt about the accident. There's one old man in robe and stocking cap who waves his arms excitedly. A group of women all relate the fall to those who weren't there. Just the house with figures dancing on the roof is still; the mother probably is riding north. A limba tapper has appeared inside the shed out back, and pours from two large gourds of wine for thirsty customers.

The sun grows cruel as the hour approaches noon. There's time enough to pay a visit to the A.D.O. A scrawny mongrel heralds my approach with two neurotic yaps, then slinks away to shun attacks.

But as I mount the first step to the porch, I realize the wife will be more distant now than ever if by chance she's caught alone. Ah, good: another voice is laughing there. I peer in, tapping, and here is Sao.

—Come in, cries Mrs. Oduram, with an excess that betrays her. Although *evoluée*, she refracts male attentiveness; she prefers to gaze away and ask of trivia— and *my* replies, at least, she never seems to hear.

Sao's just so different. She greets me in the local tongue; it's pert and I am pleased. We quickly reach my limits, whereupon she laughs infectiously. The Missus also laughs, but stridently, her eyes turned to the wall, and all too soon she comments on the heat. But here I raise my conversation piece: a devil's fall. Unhappily I fail to interest them, or so it seems, with Mrs. O's untimely laughs and Sao's puzzled glance.

I've broken up a pleasant *tête-à-tête*. It's time for lunch, providing me a reason to withdraw. Frau Oduram insists she's grateful for my call; for all I know she thinks she is, and Sao throws a grin.

The hundred yards' amble home immerses me in sweat. The house inside is cool, but soon enough the sun will penetrate my cinder walls. My steward lays on soup, a less than savvy choice; I leave the table soaking, as before.

Now, at this time of day all motion stops. The road itself grows still. In keeping with the local mode I drop into the hammock that I've strung across my porch, a book and drink at hand. It would be hard to stay awake were not the flies so thick.

A single lorry buzzes by my berth. A goat meanders up to munch gardenias I have nurtured carefully. I offer him *carte blanche*, for he will chomp those teardrop buds some other time if I deny him now. At last, at 4, a wisp of breeze comes up and things begin to move again. A limping woman, pan atop her head, and in the pan a chicken coop, comes up to stare at me. She sticks a pipe between her gums and lights it, lingering with thoughtful glance. I speak to her. Her answer shows me she is drunk.

—Coppah, Mastah, says she, left palm stretched out, right hand on top. I grin and shake my head. Twice more she makes her plea, then nods and shuffles on. The rooster in the coop is cackling stridently.

It's time I learn just how the trial is going. First a bath, a change of clothes; refreshed, I take the road. Mrs. Oduram is seen, playing with her youngest dark-eyed son; I wave, she cries—no, shrieks—"hello." A growing gathering huddles under and around the palm-wine shed; a palaver seems abuilding.

I pass by Sao's house and reach the court *barrie*, a low-walled pavilion. Here are maybe forty men and women, who watch from benches facing the Court

President, his clerk and two policemen. Seeing the interpreter before the court I step in at the back. My entrance causes flurries of unrest. Several glances come my way; a chair is called for, which I smilingly decline. Of course, I barely understand what's being said, but after several moments, Mr. Briwa heads my way, undoubtedly at court's request. He's in a more ebullient frame of mind.

—They are discussing punishment for him, he says.

A long debate ensues, for all the older men attending know, it seems, some precedent, or wish to raise a question on procedure. The calm interpreter awaits his fate, impassive, so that one would think him uninvolved. I learn the session started towards 3. They ramble on until it's almost 6, till everyone has had his say and more. The President judiciously has napped but seems to know the moment to conclude, to silence the contestants and to render his decision, that the culprit pay a three-pound fine. Mr. Briwa and the others nod their heads in sage concurrence. The miscreant advances, and gives the clerk three bills, the which, apparently, were crumpled in his fingers all this while.

Well, the fellow got his just reward, says Mr. Briwa, as we step outside. One must take better care about Goboi. And oh, he adds, I have good news for you: the dead boy is not dead.

Recalling whom he means I voice profound relief.

—Yes, he says, the mother saw him run among the trees.

—But how, I ask respectfully, could she have sent back word so soon? It was a full day's trip, correct?"

He frowns and shrugs and says he knows no more; he only knows the boy's alive but hiding in the woods. I re-affirm my happiness, as well as my opinion that the mother must be angry with her errant son. Again he blinks and frowns.

—No, he says, the woman will be joyous, for of course she loves her son.

I see it's time to part, and his unsure but sparkling smile—a flash of gold—repays my own tenfold.

The waning sun reminds me to retrace the homeward path—the Tonkolili Road. The inchoate evening coolness quickens me. I wave to Mr. Oduram; he's seated as so often in the evening playing draughts on Sao's veranda, with the chiefdom clerk, her husband. Both gaily call to me by name, at which point Sao too appears, so tempting in her yellow cloth, coquettish in her wave.

I walk on past the palm-wine shed, the quiet house beneath the dancers, last the pink and lonely bungalow.

And now—

I'm conscious of the women pounding rice;

of men returning from their farms, their matchets in their hands;

of palms and paw-paw trees, leaning languid on the dusk.

Soon the night will tumble down, engulfing Tonkolili in an enigmatic sky.

GETTING TO BO

I always said the people out in Boindu deserved a better deal. I'm talking about one family in particular, but the whole place seemed like a hard-luck village. Maybe that's why I ended up there, deep in the West African bush. I had a domestic problem back home—my impatience got me into trouble and we all needed some space. So I went where I was needed; I'm handy and I like to help out. The money was okay too. But it bothered me, what happened to folks like the Massaquois, their name was.

I was out there all alone but I made a life for myself. I had no problem with the villagers, but with the roads, the rains, the dust, the heat, it was a different story. Maybe too with the other Yanks in the aid mission back in Bo. At least, I was ready to do a job, but these guys had a hell of a time keeping me supplied. I must have spent half my time the first year either driving to Bo to pick up materials and maybe bitch a little (okay, and have a few beers with the guys so they wouldn't forget me) or getting on the radio to ask what the hell was going on. Because this trades center I was supposed to be building still existed mostly in my head.

The business of the sick miner pretty much says it all. I was waiting not real patiently for an important (well, self-important) visitor one afternoon, when I walked into the kitchen and saw Sorie standing at the big louvered window, staring at the road. We lived right on the edge of the village. I remember I'd bathed and put on a clean shirt and was rolling up the sleeves—you know, like a guy ready to go to work—and I thought Sorie had spotted Myers and his truck. Either that or the town lorry, which was bringing back food and drink from Bo.

Sorie was my steward. He'd been passed on to me by a departing aid worker who lived in the north, and he was Temne. Never mind that he'd been raised only a hundred miles away: damned if he could speak Mende, which was the language of Boindu. That's Africa. He got along with the local people and basically with me by using Pidgin, which I could "sabe," as they say, but didn't speak so well. Sorie was probably 50 himself and not very happy there. I could understand that, but he had a job to do, just like I did. Anyway, I said to him, "Lorry coming?"

"No," he said. "Miner." He didn't point, which he considered impolite.

I saw a crude litter being lugged by four men, who lowered it just at that minute, right in front of my eyes. They were hauling a big fellow I recognized, Amara Massaquoi. He'd come to me about a job just after my arrival in Boindu. I had nothing then, because I was still figuring out how to get beyond putting up the cinder-block walls and a corrugated tin roof (and running up and down the road, even in the rains), but I was impressed. You see, no adult in the village spoke fluent English except the chief and a few primary school teachers like Millie. But here was a young man who could speak well and seemed intelligent; he deserved a chance, that one. He told me he'd gone to the junior secondary school in Jimmi a couple of years until his father ran out of money to pay school fees. I gathered the old man didn't really get what a promising kid Amara was or what education could do for them all. Then came an arranged marriage and now Amara had his own kids. I asked if he was working his father's farm.

"No sir," he replied. "I'm a diamond miner." So he worked in the little stream in the forest near my house where a few alluvial diamonds had turned up over the years.

"It seems like a hard life," I recall saying. If I just had the materials I needed I could have taught him to lay pipe or told him about rebar or trained him in all the little ways I knew to make a building snug.

"Yes, it is hard," he said, "but I am a strong man, and if I find one diamond tomorrow, I can build my mother a big-big house and pay school fees for my children."

I wished him well, thinking that somehow or other I would find a suitable use for him, but there was by this time little need for anything but grunt labor until the equipment arrived. So now he lay out there coughing. The other men were catching their breath before they carried him to his home.

"Sorie," I said, "you don't have to rush chop; I'll get on the radio to ask where the 'big man' (meaning Myers) is. You go find out what's happened to that miner."

Sorie never said, "Why me?" but I could read the look on his face. He was set in his ways. I bet there were hundreds of things he disapproved of, hard as he tried not to speak about them.

I watched a moment as he went out. His greetings with the miners were not extensive; after all, Sorie was a stranger. They all looked toward the house till I moved away from the window. A few minutes later, when I was unable to get through on the radio, I watched the bearers hoist the litter again. Sorie turned toward home—expect he felt let off the hook. He was lean and not too long in the body but man, he was constitutionally long in the face.

"Is it tummy palaver?" I asked him, though I knew it wouldn't be something so simple as a belly-ache.

"Dey'ns say, na fever." Sorie bowed, maybe respectfully. "Make I fix chop now."

"Good enough. I'll try the radio again."

I remember it was Smyrnow rather than Bud Jackson who picked up the call. We hadn't spoken in months or seen each other much since my early days; he wasn't someone I gravitated to. Anyway, we chatted. How was the shop coming along? he asked.

"Fine," I said, "if I can get what I'm calling in for. You know about it? Over."

"Indirectly. Look, the chief's still here, Arnie. You know the way it is with schedules. But we're pushing as hard as we can. Over."

"Is Myers there in the office, then? Over."

"Hell no. He ain't even back from the dam site yet. Over."

Before I switched on I got rid of a few choice words. "Now he'll have a heavy rain to wade through," I told Smyrnow. "Look, does he know how bad I need that stuff? You tell him, will you? Over."

The thing was, none of those guys in Bo knew much about construction. I did. Once I wanted to be an engineer but I ended up getting a degree in construction management, even before that got to be the in thing to do. So I knew a lot about plumbing, carpentry, and electrical circuits. They even said in Washington and in Bo, too, that I was just the guy to build a center for young Sierra Leoneans, where they could be trained in the crafts.

But all I'd got done in Boindu by this time was just to set up my own living quarters and get up the walls for the center—well, and stick in the windows. I'd wired my own house, and that created quite a stir. For a few nights, neighbors would lurk outside the windows to look at the lamps and me. I wouldn't even know they were there until all at once a voice would startle me near out of my pants, calling out "Good night, Sah!" Finally I had a spontaneous party or two and let people turn the lights on and off and listen to the generator; it was fun to watch the little kids at it. Like I said, they deserved better.

And I'd done a good job with the wiring. Those circuits would have supported an electric stove—kind of ironic, because there was a wood stove in place and Sorie was used to it, even kind of fixed on it. We also had a kerosene refrigerator. I'd never seen one before but it worked well enough. I was ready to lay in plumbing too, but a steady water supply was beyond my know-how and kind of a long-term worry. Anyway, all I'd given the folks of Boindu was a little show and no substance.

So here was Smyrnow saying, "Read you loud and clear, old buddy. I know what it's like sitting out in bush alone waiting for someone to supply back-up. What's it been, a year now? Over."

"Thirteen months. The damn machinery was to be in place inside a year but I'll be lucky now just to have the main generator and switches installed by next month. And the pipes and faucets. Tell him I can't keep my men busy as it is. He'll see why I'm grousing when he gets here. Over."

"Hell of a country to do a job in, ain't it? But at least, Arnie, they tell me you don't keep none too lonely out there." And he giggled, for god's sake.

I cut him off. So they all knew about Millie. So what? Yes, I had a woman. There in Bo, they had bars and restaurants and even whorehouses if you were the type. Some of the guys had their wives with them. I didn't have a wife any longer or a buddy, just a woman to talk to. She spoke enough English, she was warm and willing, and she was using me just as much as I was using her. I couldn't trust her a lot, but even so, I liked her. She didn't ask for much—just cigarettes, and a fancy umbrella, and occasionally a few pounds to feed this apparently endless extended family of hers. Look, you did what you had to do in bush to make life work and to get things done.

I mean, should I have given Sorie a big dash (the word they used there for "tip") and sent him back to his kinfolk? After all, I suppose I had the time, given the screw-ups along the supply line, to find food for myself, chop wood for the stove, cook the food, wash my clothes, iron them, try to keep the place clean. But what use would I have been to anyone else? I just wanted to be unleashed.

I couldn't even talk about it with anyone. I didn't want to bring work problems home to a woman but I tried to with Millie—once. Who else did I have? We were in the bedroom when I looked at my watch and said I needed to get on the radio to Bo. What I should have said was, "Just wait here; I'll come back," because she was always happy enough lolling in bed. But I screwed up; she says, "You let me talk?" I tell her that's a bad idea but she can listen in— why I said it, I don't know. That breaks a little rule of mine about separating work and play. So she's there in the radio room in all her glistening splendor when I get into a discussion with the team about pipes and wiring and target dates. Without looking her way, I can see her nose turning up, and I cut the conversation a bit short.

"Why these Americans so slow-slow?" she laughs.

"There's a supply line problem," I try to explain, "and unless it's straightened out, we'll waste time and a lot of money."

"But you can relax and enjoy the life." We're back in the bedroom by this time.

"Look," say I, "I'm supposed to make a trades center run where there isn't any now, and I plan to get the job done right."

I won't get into her response, but she did have a way of changing the subject. So this time I got back on with gossipy Smyrnow and said, "Remind Bud about the steel trusses too. I've got by without them so far because my guys know all about roofing a cinderblock building. But there's no shop if I don't get machinery and wiring. Over."

"We get the message, old pal. And I'll tell Myers you got the drinks waitin', just to spur him along."

I said that once I had what I needed, Myers could get falling down drunk for all I cared. I wouldn't join in (I said to myself). There was too much of that among the expatriates—that and bitching about the local help, who could actually teach us a thing or two, truth be told. Anyway, I was ready to go to work.

So we wouldn't wait dinner for Myers, and I just hoped he'd be there by midnight. The sun went down at 7 as it always did. By nightfall the rains were pouring onto us. The Bo tarmac was 20 miles north and in between was treacherous laterite—a dust-machine in the dry months and a ski slope in the heavy rains—which, thank God, were due to let up sometime soon.

"I'll eat my chop now," I told Sorie. "Cover the rest and keep it for the big man. Then you can go rest. When he comes, we have to take care of him."

I went at my food with a vengeance, meant for Smyrnow, I guess, and Myers, and the roads. Sorie lingered or somehow showed me that, much as he hated to, he needed to tell me something. I prodded him.

He stood straight. "Miner have fever, Sah. So dem be say."

"Maybe it's malaria."

"I t'ink maybe not same fever. Be too much death, this place."

Damn, I thought, it's pneumonia. That's what the miners usually got, standing in those swamps. Why were the people of Boindu getting a trades center before they had a health clinic? "So how do you know this?"

"One lili borboh done come."

"When?"

"He dey, Sah."

"Christ, Sorie." Sure enough, I saw a little kid standing on the verandah.

Sorie disapproved. A child shouldn't be coming to speak to a big shot like me. I took a big gulp of Star beer to keep from growling at Sorie, and he slipped away.

There outside my door was this six-year-old in a ragged shirt and dirty shorts. His feet were bare, and he seemed chilled by the rain. I brought him inside. He was really alert, and cute as a kitten. I wondered how we could talk, but he said "Good evening, Sir."

"What's your name?"

"I am Moses Massaquoi, Sir."

When I asked about his English, he said he went to school and also, his father taught him; he was Amara's son. He spoke the local dialect, of course—something between Pidgin and English—but he seemed precocious. "My father is too sick, sir."

I said I was sorry.

He went on, "Can you be able go see 'un, Sir?"

"Have some of this food, " I said, "and we'll talk about that." Well, he let me think he wasn't hungry, though I was sure he was. "You see, I'm not a doctor—you know what a doctor is?"

He nodded. "But you have motor, Sir." He didn't see the need to say any more, so the ball was left right in my court. He had huge brown eyes for such a tot.

"Well, why not?" Once I had a little chap like him.

Somewhere I had a first aid kit. If Myers came, Sorie could make him welcome and give him a beer. But that left me in a bind. Because I'm thinking I have to take Sorie along to translate things this little boy won't understand. But then I say to myself, Myers is in fact my boss and I've got to stay on his good side, really play the genial host. Even if he thinks he's the grand benefactor of the African peoples, which he wasn't, though maybe he was better at it overall than I was.

Then I thought of Millie, and I don't mean, to entertain Myers. It might cheer him up, all right, but it could only be bad news for me. And for a nanosecond I considered sending Sorie to ask Millie to be ready to go with me. But no: That was the dumbest idea of all. I got a chance to see those two express affection for each other one day. Millie and I had come out of the bedroom. I was getting ready to run an errand. She was tired, she said, and would stay for a rest. "And I want some tea. Tell your boy to make it for me."

Sorie headed for the kitchen but he couldn't disappear before I caught him. Millie was my guest, after all. I said "Sorie, some tea for her highness and me."

The tea came and then she wanted food. I relayed the message and several pots banged in the kitchen. "That person is too rude," she said loudly.

"When you've had your food," I said, "please go back to the bedroom and don't bother him." I figured she'd entertain herself fingering my clothes and the pictures and knickknacks I kept on my dresser.

I told Sorie to feed her and go have his rest. But he looked at me like I'd lost my senses. "I no go go wey titi dey," he said. By golly, he was going to keep watch over the family treasures.

"Maybe you're right," I said. Millie was cute but she was capable of creating a little mischief or stealing cigarettes.

I was gone less than an hour and when I came back, it was like electricity radiating from the house. I stepped near a window but kept out of sight, to hear what was going on.

"You! Bring more tea," Millie had just said.

"You go na you 'ouse now," he said.

Millie replied that she was my woman and she would stay as long as she liked. Sorie told her that he could not leave her there alone.

"Bring tea at once, you fool!" she cried. "Just because you don't have your own woman—"

Sorie lost control and told her in two or three languages what she could do to herself.

I saw her pick up the umbrella I'd given her and come at him, but he slapped her. When she jumped away, he seized the umbrella from her hand and bent it across her back. She screamed and dropped to the floor. Opening the door he ordered her out. I backed away. After a final scream at him she scooted toward the road. I wouldn't think she could move that fast in a tight skirt and sandals, but she did. He threw the umbrella after her with some choice insults in Temne. Later, when he had gone to his room, I faked my entrance and hid the mangled umbrella until I could get rid of it in my own way.

So I got Millie an even brighter and bigger umbrella. She didn't mention the incident, but I made sure not to throw the two of them together again. She only came to me on Sorie's day off or after he had retired for the evening. It wouldn't be a good idea to send him to rouse her.

I remembered all this in about three seconds while the little boy watched. Well, he could go to Millie, while I looked for my first aid kit and read the manual a moment. It wasn't smart to ask Millie's help if she was in a highfalutin mood. But I couldn't send the boy into the rain. He'd probably been dunked in many a worse downpour, but he'd just about got dry. So I had to give in, finally. I'm a father, or I was. Calling on Millie cold looked to be the least of all evils.

I scrambled for my first aid kit. I called to Sorie that I would be back in an hour, and as an afterthought, told him there would be no food for Myers. Yes, I swiped the big boss's dinner. I carried the pot to the car and drove away with my little friend.

Moses was confused at first and tried to point me in the direction of his home. When I said I was stopping to pick up a lady, he said, "Oh, Miss Millicent Foh." Naturally. I mean, if the Americans in Bo knew about her, be sure the Mende of Boindu would, too.

When we drove up to the family compound, a teenage boy sitting in a lean-to rose without a word and went to Millie's quarters. Her family was better off than most and had a central house with a tin roof. Millie was in fact quite capable of looking down her nose at "those old native huts." There she came to her doorway, with a pout that was visible even in the faint glow of a Tilley lamp. She was that good at it, truly a Queen of Sulks. To cheer her up, I took a pack of cigarettes from the glove compartment and walked up to fetch her. "I need some help," I said.

She was dressed real nice in the West African way, wearing a head-tie, blouse, and what they called a "lappa"--I guess it meant a wrapper, usually tied at the hip. "You should send me a message," she said.

I didn't say I was sorry; somehow, apologies didn't get you anywhere with Millie.

"Is that boy in the car?" She didn't mean Moses. When I said Sorie was at home, she said it was raining hard, though it wasn't, just then.

"So get the umbrella I brought you." When she pouted again, I asked her what she had done before my arrival in Boindu—"walk between the drops?" She was yielding. I smiled and said I'd give her more cigarettes for her family. I guess I was learning to enjoy her sulks.

"What is it?" she said, hitting the last word hardest, as they did there—"What is EET?" I told her I was going to visit a sick miner. "Amara Massaquoi," she said in a flash. You just couldn't underestimate the bush telegraph.

She wasn't very happy but she was curious. We got in the car and I was charmed with little Moses's polite greeting, which she pretended not to hear; he was quite a boy. Anyway, off we went. His family lived in one of those "huts"—circular mud walls and a thatched roof. By the time we got there she was off her high horse, or at least she was enjoying a rummage in my glove compartment.

I gave Moses the pan of food to carry and picked up the first-aid kit. Under a shelter outside the hut was a small fire where the family had apparently cooked its dinner, and that was all the light we got inside. Amara Massaquoi lay restless on a mat in a corner, wrapped in a robe and stocking cap. Two women—one old, one young—kneeled near him, the younger holding a small girl; all three females seemed, even in that dim light, a bit underfed. Among several men there was an older man who stepped forward to say, "Welcome." This was the senior Massaquoi. They all seemed to be hugging themselves against the cold. It was pretty mild, of course, though after a year in mostly hot weather, even I noticed the chill of the rainy season.

The usual round of greetings followed. Then, without my saying a word, Millie began asking questions and telling me the situation. "The father says his son is very sick. They had the herbal doctor to visit but the man didn't help."

"What does that mean?"

Another man threw in, "Big palaver, Sir."

The father changed the subject. Millie translated, "He says his son is a very good man but a dreamer."

I went to Amara's side and touched his shoulder. He cried out "Aahh!," shaking me a bit. But I patted him and he looked at me and tried to say hello; little Moses crept up close to him. In a moment, Amara closed his eyes again. I put my ear to his chest, which heaved for breath. "Tell them it's pneumonia, Millie—something serious like that."

As she told them, little Moses said, "You have medicine for him, Sir?"

"Eh!" snapped Millie. "Why is this boy talking?"

"Cause it's his dad," I said. He loved his daddy all right. "No, Moses, I only have medicine to take his fever down and something to make him sleep." Millie translated. "Tomorrow morning he's got to go to the hospital in Bo."

Millie didn't look too happy with that, but she told them.

"You go take 'un, Sir?" said Moses.

Again Millie reacted, and the grandfather stepped forward with his hand drawn back. He didn't hit the boy but said, "Sorry, Sah."

"I can't, Moses." I wished I could explain about setting precedents, and running a tight ship, and the miner who would catch pneumonia next month, maybe even next week—about misusing government vehicles and all that—but this didn't seem like the time. So I said, "Millie, remind them of the lorry that goes to Bo every morning. He needs to be on it, and not in back—in the front seat." I got into my first-aid kit, took out 6 aspirin and put them in the wife's hand, but the mother took them away. I gave both women instructions, through Millie. Then I gave the father a sleeping pill—I thought I was doing the right thing—and

70

passed on more instructions. To be safe, I asked them to repeat the instructions.

"And don't forget the lorry. Oh yes, somebody needs to go with him."

The grandfather stepped forward, silenced the others, and began speaking. Millie translated: "We are very thankful you have taken the trouble to come here tonight. We know you are in Boindu to help us, and we say 'welcome.' We thank you for treating my son. God give you joy and wealth all your life."

That was a hell of a speech when I hadn't really done anything. So I said to Millie, "Just tell them likewise. Tell them I wish I could do more."

Millie jumped right in to translate.

"There'll come a time," I went on, "when people in Boindu will have medical help right away. Until then we've got to--"

Thunder rolled, causing Amara to give a hoarse cry, scaring most of us and probably himself. "Until then," I started again, "we have to look out for each other." I shook some hands, whispered good-bye to Amara, and rubbed Moses's head. Then I took Millie's arm.

"Your pan, Sir." Moses tried to give the pot of food back. So I spent another minute explaining that this food was special and that the whole family should take some.

"I don't think whether they will like it."

"Tell them medicine is supposed to taste bad." That was a good line; I wish I'd thought of it before. They all needed a good meal. Millie went along with the game, Grandpa took the food, and then we were in the car.

"How do I get out of here?" I said. "I'm a little lost." I turned on the lights and she pointed the way. "Okay. I'll turn around, but watch so I don't run over anyone." The whole extended family, it seemed, was outside looking on.

On the way to her compound, I commented that this was a hell of a business.

"Where are you taking me?" was her reply.

"To your place."

"So early?" There came that pout again. It may have been one of her main attractions for the men of Boindu, but I managed to disengage.

"I gotta get back. The boss man may be there now with my supplies."

"Every time big-big hurry," she said, "then nothing to do."

What a hoot! She was right as rain, and now I can laugh about it, but then I was a bit pissed. "I make big-big money because of my big-big hurry, Sweetheart, and you should be glad of that."

"You going to give your Millie a special present?"

"I gotta do something for you. You were great in there." And so she was. I always said, it wasn't the people that caused the problems (at least, not the Africans), just everything in the environment. "That family must be some worried, but they treated me like a v.i.p."

"So what you do for me?"

"But if the old man had hit Moses, I'd have been mad."

"That boy was too rude."

"What is it with you folks, that you don't let kids ask questions?" And it was true. Moses was the only small kid I saw in Sierra Leone that might be called assertive. "What was Grandpa upset about, anyway?"

"You don't understand about palaver?" she said.

"Tell me."

"They couldn't pay the herbalist, so he left."

"I figured it might be that."

"Although they say they will put this Amara on the lorry, but I don't think whether there is money."

"Look," I said, "there are some things people have to do. And I can't do everything. In fact, I may be finally getting this project off the ground."

I pulled up at her compound. She was in no hurry to get out. "Tell Millie what you're going to give her," she said.

"Tell you what. I'll take you to Bo and we'll have a fine time."

"Tomorrow?"

"No, not tomorrow. I told you. If I get the stuff I need, I'll have a big day's work tomorrow." Whatever my faults, the soft and easy life was not for me. I didn't want to feel like a parasite.

At 7:45 the next morning I sent in my first call. Bud Jackson responded a few minutes past eight, saying "You all right, Arnie?"

"Morning, Bud. I'd have slept better if my company had come. Over."

"Arnie, we tried to call last night and couldn't get you and didn't have another chance. Anyway, he had a change of plans. Over."

"Look, Myers can change any plan he damn pleases but not my plan. Is he bringing me my generator and joiners and wiring or isn't he? Over."

"Well, it doesn't look so good but we're working out our options, fair enough? I'll pass you the word after I've talked with him. Over."

"Call in about 12:30, okay? I'm still trying to do a decent day's work out here. Over and out."

I was getting into the Jeep, muttering to myself, when I heard the sound of a motor. The morning lorry was leaving for Bo. I walked to the road and flagged it down. It was a five-ton truck with a pretty typical slogan—"No Man Like God"—painted on its frame. I greeted the driver, stepped onto the running board, and looked in. The people in the front seat with him were strangers. I went to the back, where twenty more strangers stared at me over their goats and chickens and bags of grain.

"Sorie," I called as I neared the house. Maybe I should have driven to the Massaquois' hut myself, but my workmen were waiting and I didn't want them to get the idea we didn't keep regular hours on this job. I figured we could start installing light-fixtures on the structure we'd got up (since I didn't know what else to have them do). Sorie came to the doorway and I didn't try to talk Pidgin; I just said, "The miner wasn't on the truck. Today you have to go to his place and find out why. Find out how he's doing, too." I was trying to bend Africa to my will.

Anyway, Sorie gave me his "Why me?" look and went back inside and I drove off to install light fixtures without wires. The fixtures had been sent out months ago but none of the wiring had reached Bo until the week before, and it was going to be delivered by a touring mission chief who couldn't keep to his schedule. So I directed my two-man crew in loosely installing fixtures that would probably have to be taken off again when it was time to connect the wiring.

When I came home, Sorie was slowly getting lunch on. "What about that miner?" I said.

Sorie told me he hadn't had time to go but would walk into town during the afternoon.

"Think you'd have time to get out of the house if it caught fire?" I said. He didn't understand and maybe I didn't want him to. I set about eating my food. The meat was always tough out there, so you couldn't engage in any fastidious conversations. Twelve-thirty came with no radio, so I swallowed the gristle and went to the shack. Pretty soon Jackson said, "Bo reading you, Boindu. I hadn't forgotten. Over."

"We're having a hot old time out here today, Bud. I've put in 15 light fixtures without wiring. Maybe you'd like to send me the lathes and drills so I can put them in without wiring too. Over." I didn't mention the fact that I'd put one of my guys to work adding shims to window frames that were already pretty firmly in place.

"You're getting wiring and the generator both, the whole works, today. Fair enough? Over."

I asked if Myers was coming.

"No, he's going to see a chief who's somebody's brother and then he's flying back. But I've got a driver due in from Kenema who'll be on his way out this afternoon, I guarantee it. Over."

"Before my crew knocks off? Over."

"No promises on that. We gotta load the stuff, you know. Over."

"Look, I need him to come out here and go back into Bo tonight. I'll give him a dash. And one more thing, Bud. Ask the sawbones to stick in something for respiratory problems, probably pneumonia. Ask him to trust me. Over."

"You're all right, aren't you, Arnie? That place isn't getting to you? Over."

"Yeah, it is. I don't like people younger than me dying. They don't seem to like it either and there are a few pressures, know what I mean? Send me some terramycin or whatever and tell your driver to expect a long day. Over."

"It's a deal—"

I interrupted with my switch before he could blab on. "Listen Bud, I'll come in with the Jeep if I have to, and if the coils are too large to fit around the generator I'll recoil the goddam wires around the outside. It's that bad. Over."

"Arnie, would I let you down?"

We signed off and I got ready to go back to work. I told Sorie he had to get to the Massaquois' place, no excuses, and this time I said it in Pidgin. There were a couple of principles involved here, obvious to most people but maybe not to him. Anyway, it was one o'clock, the time school let out, so I drove past Millie's to tell her I was going to be too busy to see her for a day or two. I met her walking up the road and got out to give her the news. But then, I said, we'd have ourselves a time. She kind of liked being seen with me in broad daylight. I guess I was a catch.

"You're the big man," she said. "Why you can't find time for Millie?"

There wasn't much to say to that. She was a lot younger than I was, and unlike most of the women around there, she looked good in a European-style dress. I wanted to take her to the house but it was working hours and here was another principle I tried to follow.

So I set my crew to looking for cracks and sealing them with mortar, though they knew as well as I did that the place was perfectly snug. I made a note to ask for more carpentry tools and wondered what else we'd do if Bud's driver didn't pull up soon. Finally I drove back to the house to see about him. Sorie was there, alone. I guess I should have known.

I had to ask Sorie about Amara. I don't know if he'd have said anything otherwise. "Dey'ns no want talk Temne man," he complained. He added that Boindu was a bad place.

"But they did talk, didn't they?"

"Borboh done come."

I waited.

"Ask too many questions."

"Well, how is the miner?"

The miner was feverish—of course. Sorie had relayed the message that Amara needed to go to Bo. Moses then asked him why I didn't send my car. A smart boy, that one, and doing his all for his dad.

"I tell 'un Mastah say he dey come just now."

And I might just check in, Moses, I was thinking. That instant, I saw him walking up the road, carrying my saucepan. "Here's the little fellow now."

"Pickin dey talk like big-big man," said Sorie. He slipped away, unable to face the boy's bad behavior. I went out onto the verandah.

Black clouds had come up again to the north. Moses moved right up the road and got in my face, sort of--not meeting my gaze, which was considered rude in Boindu. I can see him now, in my mind's eye. He held out the pan but he'd really come so as I would bring my car. Well, I told him, I was going to do better than that.

So I showed him the radio room and had him listen in while I called about the truck and the terramycin. And he gets to hear my temper boil when Smyrnow tells me the driver gave up on the road and turned back. Good thing for Smyrnow we talked before I walked out and saw "No Man Like God" coming up the road, covered with mud up to its bed but doing what the people of Boindu needed it to do. Moses got to hear a few more bad English words.

Then I had to go to the work site and tell the men they could knock off early. A bad precedent, of course. Moses in his own polite way was pressing me but I know it wasn't even an hour before we got to the hut. I heard an eerie wailing but it stopped when I got out of the car. He heard it too and he ran ahead of me. Inside they were all gathered around the inert form of Amara Massaquoi. I bent down to touch him, took his wrist, ground my teeth, and the wailing went up to a terrifying volume. I took hold of Moses' arm. Grandpa reached over to touch me and said, "T'ank you, Sah." I almost swatted him. Why would he say that? Damn: how could he thank me?

THE LEGEND OF DEATH'S STAIRCASE

(Reprinted from *The Antigonish Review 145* [Spring 2006], 87-94)

A headless staircase once stood on *l'ile de Gorée*—in the harbor at Dakar—suspending itself over the sea. Its origins were doubtless prosaic enough, but in the mind of a Henry Lovell its bulky aspiration toward the stratosphere might easily compel fantasies of otherworldly purposes. It could be found on the seaward shore of the island, facing the spindly Dakar peninsula: a flight of fifteen and more concrete steps climbing only to a small landing hovering over the ocean. For years it was no more than a curiosity to the traveler who happened onto Goree. Then in 1962, the Lovells gave to it the legend that has since cloaked it in Gothic misapprehensions.

Although they had lived in Dakar several years and spoke good French, the Lovells were not French *colons*, as is sometimes claimed, but American expatriates. Information about their lives became available at the time of the event, owing particularly to Mary Lovell's gregarious frankness. Henry was engaged in research on French expansion into the West African interior and subsequent rule from the colonial capital—a study which, although unfinished, is considered (by his colleagues and mine) a somewhat substantial contribution to the understanding of the region's history. He was forty-five at this time but still a youthful figure in his customary white shirt and slacks. Only eyes shaded by his long struggle with depression— recently exacerbated by his wife's illness and perhaps other factors—gave away his age. Mary Catherine Lovell ("M.C." to her friends) had worsened and looked older, though one knew, as she did, that she had been lovely.

The couple lived a comfortable life and were financially well off. About the time the Ford Foundation grant that had brought them to Dakar ran out, they found themselves each coming into inheritances that could keep them there comfortably. They lived in a charming white bungalow rented from the Simca distributor, who was more than happy to have a quiet "European" couple as permanent tenants. The house was small but sunny and situated to capture breezes even in the dry season. Behind was a well-tended garden colored by a procession of bougainvillea, frangipani trees, the famous African flame trees, a profusion of flowers. Mary Catherine could often be found there, reading on a bench or on the outdoor furniture where they infrequently entertained friends and associates.

They had met at college. Henry was a serious graduate student and M.C. a socially-minded sophomore. Both were well-liked. Contemporaries lodged no complaint against Henry, except for the annoyance of his great unselfconscious sighs—"a cross," said one, "between a yawn and a scream." His popularity—good looks and a boyish way of running his hand through his hair and smiling—belied his depression. "It's his father," M.C. told friends, without explanation. There was little more she could say except that she was glad she was not the focus of her husband's anger. She found his father pleasant and reliable. Not so, Henry: she hinted that filial anger as much as an abiding research interest had driven Henry into expatriation.

The couple had no children. Their lack of issue bothered Lovell, who wanted to leave his name behind when he died. But M.C. had chosen to remain childless. She said she was too spoiled, and was quoted as confessing, "Oh, I was afraid pregnancy would spoil my figure." In her twenties she had done a little modeling—not for the great fashion houses, to be sure, but enough to lift her chin in later years. She knew she lacked Henry's intellectual discipline, as well as the drive to carry out a professional career; her infallible talent for looking good must be her own gift to the world. For emotional companionship she had chosen a string of pets, the last of which had recently died.

She had come to Africa reluctantly, but then discovered the pampering that expatriates could command in that immediate post-colonial era. There were a steward, a night watchman, and a gardener to cater to all of her wishes, or all but one: The servants disliked dogs and neglected to care for her pets. She adjusted to their failings and liked the servants anyway. Overall she found the luxury irresistible. She had little enough to do, but she stayed active reading American magazines, polishing her French, and getting to know the Senegalese merchants in the market. No one there thought her beautiful. She was *trop maigre;* the Senegalese advised her to fatten up. She didn't mind their gentle criticism. One part of her had always disliked the leers of her countrymen. Once adjusted to the shock of her 40th birthday, she became quite cheerful about her status as a slender older woman who could still wear clothes well and flaunt a mane of blond hair.

Slowly her French overtook Henry's despite his long head start, for she had mastered all the registers except perhaps that found in French intellectual discourse. He proved no match for her in speaking with the French merchants who cultivated Parisian elegance and liked *l'americaine* for dressing after their fashion, and he left dealings with their landlord strictly to M.C. Those *negociants* who withstood her charm took advantage of them—she handled decisions poorly and gave in too easily—but others, including the Simca distributor, were virtually seduced by her and did her favors. Her letters to her sister and nephews were full of adventure and good cheer, except that she grieved when one of her pets died. As for Henry, it could not be determined whether he enjoyed their privileged life together or was simply blocked by his depression from moving on. Despite growing signs that M.C.'s illness required radical intervention, for example, he clung to Dakar rather than break loose.

It is now possible to trace the events of the day in question. They took the regular launch out from the city to Goree on this September Saturday not in spite of, but because of, the likely heavy rains that fall at this time of year. During even the brief span of their crossing they had sensed the wind's rising, the growing brawl of the waves, the portents of the storm.

Upon arrival, Henry led her immediately to the old slave quarters beneath a large Spanish-style house on the mainland side of Goree. Perhaps they stayed too long inside: he fell into a deep fit of withdrawal, one of those spells when he became unfathomable. More than M.C.'s health weighed on him. The journals in our field were beginning to treat his research as a dead end, to reject his manuscripts. Scholars of the day wanted historical work on African peoples and states rather than French colonialism. In the absence of indigenous records, modern researchers were turning to the newly devised technique of oral history. Henry disparaged history that could not be documented, but once admitted, with the candor that made him likable, "I'd be a flop at interviewing chiefs and elders anyway," as he smiled and ran his hand through his hair.

In any case, one must imagine him paralyzed by the ambiance of those dank, dark cells where men were once consigned to spend their days, with no headroom even for a man of medium height, and no outlet except to the sea.

"Enough," M.C. said at last. "Let's not stay here. It's not worth thinking of."

Almost reluctantly, he led her out. They returned in the direction of the dock, to the ancient esplanade, and past its frontal balustrade to the shore, where they could glimpse the staircase and the city across the bay. The sun was shining but dark clouds had begun massing above the sea.

"It is terribly strange," she said. Oddly, she had never before visited Goree, perhaps thinking of it as squalid and depressing. M.C. was not one for contemplating African poverty. "You haven't let it get you down, have you?"

"Remember," Lovell replied, missing her question, "it has to be seen close-on, and in the rain, to be appreciated."

M.C. resisted flights of fantasy. "It's just a staircase leading to the top of a staircase," she laughed. From its appearance, it might have been the support of a bridge that once joined Goree to Dakar but had been broken into pieces,

"It's more than that," Lovell insisted. Yet he refused as he always had to explain what it was that struck him so, that—apparently—awed him. "Let's have our lunch. We'll come back later."

As usual, M.C. was not hungry, but she quickly agreed; she wanted to sit down and wanted for him the lift in spirits that meals usually brought him. He was at least borderline hypoglycemic and tended to become cross when his food was delayed.

He helped her down the slow incline below the esplanade. Beneath them, by the dock, there was a crumbling, gray-faced restaurant where they could take their meal.

"This is an eerie little town, certainly," she said, "But you—with your penchant for the mysterious, you make it sound like a playground for witches and goblins." She wished he would smile.

"Perhaps it is. It must be." He heaved a great sigh. "The houses do look haunted, don't they? And the slave quarters would be the perfect home for angry spirits."

"Your imagination is the perfect home," she said, gripping his arm.

Lovell was watching her. "You aren't sorry we came—?"

She placed her hand on his, which held her arm, "It doesn't matter; I'm grateful just to be out walking with you." And so she managed to stay cheerful despite her malaise.

Different in mood, they were nevertheless a compatible couple. Apparently neither had ever had a liaison elsewhere. They had often spoken happily of the esthetics of sex, but neither was driven, and Henry now endured celibacy without complaint. M.C. confessed as much in a letter to her sister, as a subtle means of informing the family of her deteriorating health. If true, her confession speaks eloquently to Lovell's paralysis and his tendency to bottle up pain that needed addressing.

They entered the restaurant and seated themselves among a handful of holiday-makers. Through a small window on a level with their chins they could see the clouds preparing a watery ambush. The busy French proprietress handed them menus. She responded to M.C.'s smile with perfectly polite words in a perfectly business-like manner.

"Please take what you would most like," Henry told her. "It won't be haute cuisine but pretend, and indulge yourself."

"I'd like you to choose for me," she said. "You know me well enough."

"Then let's share chateaubriant." Lovell's words were unexpectedly tender. She knew it would be too much food, but perhaps he would like a large share of the steak.

They spoke briefly of friends, in particular of a couple who were separating. The rains came with their food and cut visibility to the end of the pier close by. The launch docked again later and rocked heavily against the pilings, for the ocean seemed as thunderous as the storm.

"It's going to be perfect for our tour," she said, smiling. He tried to smile too, but his effort pained her. His depression didn't seem to be bipolar; she had rarely glimpsed anything resembling a manic episode. But his gloom, which he managed to hide from most others, troubled their marriage as little else did. In spite of her decline, it seemed that Henry suffered more.

He showed little interest in his food. "M.C., I hope," he said, "I hope," and his voice seemed caught, "I hope you don't mind going through with this—?"

She frowned, "It's beginning to seem a little macabre. We should be doing very gay things, you know. When I feel better, why don't we take another trip to Nice?"

He stared at her. "That would be great, but—"

"But Goree will have to do."

He chose not to understand her. "It's why we came."

"Yes," she said, "it's why we came." She looked outside, thinking, what a different mood rain brings. Henry of course was just as cheery in the rain as in the sun, if "cheery" was ever a word that could apply to him.

"Shall we go, then?"

"Now? You haven't eaten enough."

"Nor have you. Don't let me rush you."

"As usual, I don't have much appetite. But you're the one who's always hungry."

He shook his head. "Not this time. Are you ready?"

After finishing her wine she nodded, and he settled the bill with the proprietress, who hoped they would come back, even as she made it clear she knew they were foreigners. They draped themselves in plastic raincoats and hats—M.C., who chilled easily, first pulled a sweater over her thin white blouse—and walked into the downpour. It was a relentless rain characteristic of the Coast, as distinct from the rains of moderate climes: not so much a welcome visitor as a gritty relative who comes to stay. If she was less than enthusiastic, M.C. managed to hug Lovell's arm to her breast as they set off. At 42, her features were notably fine except for the sallow cast of her eyes and skin. Five months before, she had experienced the first signs of debilitation, a certain lethargy and a creeping, irksome listlessness. When she began losing weight they made a visit to the States; later they went to Germany, and finally to France, but they found medical institutions in the Western world deficient at that day in their understanding of rare tropical diseases. One specialist offered a diagnosis of fibromyalgia, but retracted it because M.C. laughed several times as they spoke, and almost seemed to be enjoying herself. At first the two of them pretended that no news was good news, but time had taught them better: She grew slowly weaker.

Already the rain had turned the earth to mire. They stayed with the narrow street that wandered toward and through the houses, unconsciously hurrying as though in search of shelter. Lovell grew quiet, distracted. She could sense the tension in his biceps, where her fingers were resting. She would be glad when the day had ended.

As they once more entered the little island town, a striking Senegalese girl abruptly rounded a corner and ran toward them, startling Lovell. She wore no raincoat but tried vainly to make a small umbrella protect her, her body writhing with her stride. Lovell slowed his pace and stared after her.

"Quite a beauty." M.C. smiled. "Wouldn't you say?"

Lovell looked at his wife as if surprised. "Oh—yes I suppose so."

"I thought you observed very carefully."

He shook his head, hurrying on. "I didn't expect to find any one else up here today."

Although it was not easy for her, she kept pace with him. She wanted to whisper to him but had to talk loudly in order to be heard above the splatter of rain on the cobblestones. "Henry, I was so pleased that you found me an attractive bride." Why, she surely wondered, was she begging for a compliment in a domain in which she had always felt self-confident?

"You've always been a beautiful woman."

"Don't be sentimental. The Senegalese think I'm all bones, which is getting close to the truth. I just hope that when we come to the end you'll remember me the way I was then—?"

"Let's not talk about it."

She winced, thinking he was right. "Sure. We should talk about our farewell visit to Nice."

Lovell had paused now, beside the small cathedral, which gleamed a glossy yellow. "Could we go in?" he said.

She didn't mind: She was breathless, and thought it would be pleasant to escape the rain. Besides, she rather believed in God, who had always been so good to her. But then, why was He letting her body break down when she was still young?

Inside they found a lofty but vacant nave leading to a dominant but not imposing altar. The church was dark and the rain created a din above their heads. "How dreary," she commented. She had water in her shoes. "Sorry, God," she thought, "but You're making things tough."

"Churches are, in the rain," Henry responded. "Would you care to sit in a pew for a moment?"

"Thank you. I would."

"M.C, I'm going to pray—if I can."

She was startled, and touched, as he knelt in the aisle facing the altar. Lovell was not a religious man but intently irreligious: Lowering himself to his knees for god or man was unlike him and almost unbecoming. She watched apprehensively, and said a little prayer for him.

"Come on, God, assure me," he said. She waited but that was the entirety of his prayer, although he remained kneeling briefly. When he rose she embraced him.

"There's something more certain," he sighed, holding her loosely. "God in heaven," he whispered.

"Now you're dwelling on it," she said. "Why make us both unhappy?" She held him tighter until he moved gently away.

"You don't understand yet." Lovell led her slowly to the doorway, where they viewed through the scattered droplets off the lintel the wave of droplets ahead. Her head lay against his chest; she hung limply in his arms, exhausted.

"It's time," he said. "I don't understand it but I feel it has to be. Come, Dear."

She stiffened. "No," she said, "Let's go back."

Lovell seemed transfigured. "It's just a few steps."

"No, it's sinister."

"You must." He pulled her into the rain. "You'll be glad I brought you."

"I've changed my mind," she said, holding back. "Please, it's so wet and I'm tired."

His hushed voice was barely audible above the rain. "You once said it didn't matter how tired you were, that you were going to resist it as long as you possibly could."

That was when she expected to go back to Nice, she thought, and when he had promised not to obsess on her illness. But she made no answer; unwillingly, she was led on, "Please," she said.

"We must go on. There—there it is." He pulled her strongly, "Hurry. We'll just be a moment. Look at it! Have you ever seen anything so—"

She kept up as best she could, not looking at the steps, keeping her eyes down and away from the pelting rain. Her heart was lurching. Oblivious to the storm, Lovell was moving forward irresistibly.

The ocean smashed into the rocks beside them as he drew her, head still lowered, up the glistening concrete steps. At the top he put his arm around her. "Look, Darling," he shouted above the wind: "What do you see?"

She looked into an impenetrable mist; she saw nothing; the city might have been a thousand miles away. "There's nothing to see," and she urged him to take her home.

"There's everything!" He held her tight. "It will come; not blindingly, but—"

What was he suggesting? She put her hand over her mouth.

"I was here at the museum the day Moreau admitted he had no diagnosis, remember?" Lovell's words sounded distant in the wind, "Do you know, M.C. what I saw in the fog that day? I saw a beautiful hand beckoning to me."

"Take me back, Henry." Doubtless she began to weep, but the wind and the ocean muffled all sounds.

"Watch for it, my dear. It will come again today— you'll see."

She writhed in his grasp but only briefly, less afraid than aggrieved at what was happening to the man whose life she had shared. She looked up, into his brilliant eyes. Perhaps indeed he was capable of mania, but if so, he was her maniac.

The Senegalese girl returned from her errand at this moment and cried out, vainly amid the great roar of nature. Her witness should have put paid to all the speculation, but credulous people will believe what they want to believe, and that is precisely what happened.

HANDING OVER IN NUPÉ

Having left Shirin her instructions in careful detail, Mahmoud Alieu strode from his verandah to the roadside to compose his thoughts and await his ride. First, he thought, Nigel Britten would not violate her privacy with his gaze nor, second, offend her ears with his loud English, nor third, loose his smelly breath into her home—not a one of those. Alieu squatted comfortably on his heels beneath a frangipani tree, thinking. *Of course he'll go soon, but then there's that chief. Malen doubtless resisted the eviction of the colonial regime, because he liked playing emir in this soulless place. And there's Mayode: they say the revolution eats its own but he'll find out I'm not edible.* He reached beneath his Kanuri fez to scratch his head.

Britten came roaring out of the driveway of the expatriate—Hawkins or some such name—who was Mahmoud's nearest neighbor, and skidded up beside the frangipani tree. "There you are, Mahmoud," he said. "Let's be off, shall we?" *He apparently likes this place.*

Mahmoud stared straight ahead as they hurtled along in the cooperatives van, past heap after heap of laterite, perhaps thirty in all, meant to be graded over the ruts created by the long rainy season of the Niger valley. Britten, talking, let the wheels drift in the direction of the heaps but managed to miss them, and they arrived safely at the Jolima provincial offices. "This is it," he said, and for the moment before they opened their doors, the smell of beer permeated the cab. Collecting his *riga*, Alieu stepped down from the little truck to stand looking at a low-lying, tin-roofed building with a row of four open shutters.

"Coming?" Britten said.

He marched up the three steps into the Cooperatives Office, and accepted the open door that Britten with an elaborate gesture provided him. The room lacked geometry: the walls and ceiling wriggled and sagged, the floor was lumpy, and the three timeworn desks seemed to have been scuffling among themselves for space. Squeezed against one corner was a wooden honeycomb full of perhaps 15 worn, discolored files. A small Bida brass bowl served someone as an ashtray.

Britten said, "Well here it is, what there is of it. It's nothing fancy, but then we're not out to impress people. These are my inspectors; *Ka u*—stand up, chaps and meet . . . a new man who's come to work with us."

Alieu took notice of the two men who rose wordlessly to their feet, offering them a slight nod. He decided he would speak Hausa with them after today.

"Yaya here," Britten said, indicating a small wide-eyed man of about 40 dressed like his supervisor in shorts and knee-length socks, "has been with me six years. Karimu's new, but he's settling in all right. Our third man is Mr. Aloye, who is out on tour this week—and just as well, because there's no place for Karimu when we're all in. Sit down, chaps. In fact I don't know quite where to put you, Mahmoud. If I'd had a bit of notice I could have done better by you, of course."

Alieu observed a car being parked near the office next door.

"That's the provincial veterinarian," said Britten. "Would you care to meet him?"

He shook his head. Gesturing towards Karimu, he suggested that a chair could be borrowed from the veterinarian.

After a lingering glance Britten said, "Right you are; Karimu, that's a good lad." Karimu almost soundlessly left the office. He wore a *Nupé* robe and sandals; Alieu noticed that his teeth were stained from kola nuts or cigarettes. The other man, Yaya, sat rigid in his chair.

"You'll be wanting to look at the books, I expect." Britten poked through the pigeonholes, extracting files here and there. "I'll tell you this much, you'll find them all in good order. These lads have been pretty well trained." He smiled at Yaya, who lowered his eyes.

Karimu appeared in the doorway, tucking his robe aside with one hand, and holding a chair in the other. Alieu, having gathered up his *riga*, was all but seated, when he paused. "If this man is not busy, perhaps he will take this chair and let me use his desk." *Strange: 4 men, 3 chairs; can't he count? I won't try to understand him.*

"Very well, then," Britten said slowly. "It's true, he's not overly busy at the moment. Just a lull, of course, because the farmers will be harvesting next month, and then we'll be out with the *hakimis*. That's what we call the local chiefs, of course; you speak Nupe—no? Well." He seemed surprised. "That's the best part of it, you know—getting out with the local big men and the farmers and working over their accounts. One feels a great naturalness there." He added, "I suppose there's something about bush that gets into your blood."

Alieu opened an account book without responding. *This bush is not in my blood, and certainly not in yours. And this is 1965, not 1940.*

"These lads stay busy enough, have no fear. They're my loan collectors, and it's not always easy to get your money back from farmers hereabouts. *U de wahalla*, eh, Karimu? Oops—sorry, Mahmoud. They're in bush more than I am, you see. I visit most of the primary societies no more than twice a year, and one of the visits I must admit is simply for the pleasure of it—to keep up good relations." Britten's words poured out with little pause; he shifted from one leg to the other. "We have a few places I can't get into with my kit-car, of course. I have to take in five bearers when I go to Gwama, but frankly I wouldn't miss it. A fine old chief out there, Chief Audu. I use my bearers to carry out his cotton; it keeps the old man happy."

Alieu glanced away. "No doubt," he said.

He saw Britten wet his lips and frown. A breeze newly arrived off the savannah not far north banged a shutter, which Britten re-opened while the two inspectors ponderously looked on. The room had only two glassless windows, which provided both light and air; there was no electricity.

Britten turned back, his eyes on the floor. "It may seem a bit irregular," he said, "but the cooperative idea still hasn't got hold back there, and it might never do, as cut off as they are, except with the Chief's encouragement. What I ask for he sees that I get. Not a single loan outstanding in Gwama last year, you know."

Mahmoud opened a file cover to peer with feigned intensity at the contents. *The government runs the cooperative program for the benefit of the farmers, not that of the chiefs.*

"In any case, the system works." Britten turned to the two inspectors. "I believe these chaps will bear me out on that, won't you?"

"Yes sir," both men said.

Alieu looked up. "What's your name again?" he asked the small one.

"Yaya, sir."

"I find that I have forgotten my portmanteau. I want you to go quickly to my house—you know by this time where it is, I think: the former so-called European section? Good. Ask my boy to give it to you."

He watched Yaya hesitate.

Britten was a tall angular man, dressed in a shirt and shorts that might have been clean a week before. "It's all right. Go along with you, Yaya."

"Quickly now," Alieu added. "It is already 27 minutes past 8." He glanced at Karimu, whose gaze fell to the ledger before him.

Watching Yaya leave, he noticed a grid map by the door. "This is the district, is it?" He walked over to peer closely at it.

"That's right," Britten replied. "Extends about 50 miles to the north, not so far in the other directions."

"Here is Gwama"—he pointed to a small dot well to the north of the slightly larger dot that represented the chiefdom seat of Jolima. "Since it's on the river that runs through Jolima, why don't you go in and out by boat?"

"Because the Kpara is rather a small stream up there, particularly by December. You couldn't transport the cotton down by dugout very easily, if that's what you're thinking."

"If it's small, why don't they build a bridge?"

"It's not that small, and why should they, frankly? There's nothing but bush on the other side."

Alieu was silent a moment. "This is a motor road, I believe?"

Britten's eyes scaled his forefinger. "That's right. I leave my van here and trek in." He put his finger slightly beneath Alieu's.

"How far is it—three or four miles?"

"Almost five, actually."

He turned away and walked slowly to his seat. "They could build a track sufficient for the van."

"It wouldn't make a great difference," Britten said. "They're a bit slow getting things in to the warehouse but it all arrives eventually."

Alieu gazed into a file. "The waste of two days getting into that village and out again would make a difference. Perhaps these inspectors"—he waved toward Karimu—"need supervision."

"They do their jobs," Britten said. He seated himself at his desk.

They were separately at work when Yaya returned with the portmanteau; Alieu nodded shortly. Britten apparently noticed that he was checking the Mara accounts and came to stand over his shoulder.

"The bookkeeping out in the primary societies is on the crude side, Mahmoud, but you should have seen what it was nine years ago when I was posted here. You'll notice too that we've made a profit over the last four years. A lot of the credit goes to the people and the chief here, too. Have you met the *Gitsu Nupé*,Chief Malen yet?"

"Of course." *I am a Nigerian, I know to pay my respects to the local chief.*

"Grand chap, the Chief. He's been very good to me you know—one of the reasons I've felt content here." Britten glanced sharply at him.

Alieu nodded and turned away.

"This permanent secretary—you know Mayode, I expect?—might have given me advance notice of your coming, don't you think?"

As if Mayode cared about either of us—thinks he's a modern man with his telephone and calculator and clerks with typewriters and his big decisions, but he will not survive the next revolution. "Perhaps the mails have gone astray," he said.

Britten walked over to a window and gazed at the whited dust outside. "Oh, I get all the letters I don't want, Mahmoud." He looked at Yaya and Karimu, both lost in thought. "To work, Lads."

Alieu closed the account book and said, "Karimu, let us see what sort of inspections you've been making. Show me your reports."

Karimu looked at Britten, then at Alieu before obeying. None of them spoke. Alieu concluded that he had made a reasonable start in taking charge: one, two, three. If Mayode forced him to live a time in a desolate *Nupé* village, he would work hard, and in so doing, perhaps, he would avoid homesickness.

At 9:30 Britten rose to his feet and said, "Well Mahmoud, it's breakfast time. I'll give you a lift home in my kit-car."

"I had breakfast at sunrise. I prefer to stay on and review the files." He too rose but only to look at the map on the wall. "I will make my own way to home and back."

Britten gazed at Alieu a moment. This suddenly important man in his life wore a starched striped riga that seemed as though it would never wrinkle. Through his slim, erect bearing, he contrived to look as tall as Britten himself, but he was actually two-three inches shorter. Britten said no more but walked out, Yaya and Karimu at his heels.

His little van responded faithfully to his touch and he drove up the hill to his home, frowning. After parking the car beneath his giant thorn-tree he walked into the house and called, "Adamu!"—a signal to his steward to bring beer. Adamu brought the bottle and glass on a tray before Britten had seated himself. He was wearing his usual shorts and a shirt Britten had given him years earlier. "Thank you," Britten said. Adamu was a Hausa who spoke no *Nupé*, and they communicated best in a sort of primitive English.

Adamu lingered rather than return to the kitchen. He had been with Britten for 11 years. He said, "They say there be new man in your office, sir."

Britten rolled his eyes up from his glass. "So the word's out already, is it?" he said, after finishing his draught. "Well, they're right. I'm going to see the chief about him at eleven."

Adamu gazed at the ceiling, evidently concerned but inarticulate, a gentle and even passive man with a large, bristling mustache. When he failed to speak, Britten said, "Come, did you fetch the mail?"

"Yes sir." Adamu handed him an airgram.

"From the Missus again? What do you suppose she wants?"

"Money, Sir," Adamu replied on cue. He laughed softly and retreated to the kitchen. Britten realized that the little joke they shared was not fair to the woman who was still legally his wife, but this was no time to undertake changes.

Putting Mary's letter unopened onto the sideboard, Britten relaxed with his beer and gazed around his untidy parlor. The sideboard, saloon chairs, an assortment of *Nupé* carved stools, the fridge, and his dinner table, all were jumbled together in the big main room like vegetables on a local farm. He had lived there nine years. Mary had lasted two of them. He picked up her letter but put it down again.

"Hello Adamu," he called. "Hold off a little on breakfast and bring another beer."

Pacing the room, he reflected on the comforts of home: The cinder-block walls kept the heat out, the gaps beneath the eaves let the air in, the thatch above the tin roof dulled the rain. He drank strongly from the second bottle. When Adamu came in to lay the table, he unobtrusively inspected his steward from head to toe.

He seated himself to breakfast a few minutes later and ate in silence. His fried bread and an egg remained when he was done. Rising again he looked at his watch and started involuntarily before remembering that he was calling on the Chief. "Hello, Adamu," he said but then decided not to have another beer yet.

He walked to a rear window and took in ten miles of hilly terrain. He had seen leopards out in the hills through his field glasses (though not for several years) and once, as he and Hawkins sat drinking shandies on a brilliant evening, he had made a rare sighting of white stork in migration. Those were the days. The club stayed open most of the day and all evening, right through the 'fifties, and he and his chums played lively games of billiards and darts as the drinks flowed. He thought it a good life.

Adamu wiped off the ornate stool that served as drinks table. He seemed to be waiting. "Adamu," Britten said, "you should know that I may be leaving Jolima."

The steward frowned, uncomprehending. "But I think—I think you will come back—?"

"The man simply came," Britten said, looking away. "He had his letter from Mayode with him."

Before he was permanent secretary, Mayode had made a brief visit to Britten's home for a drink, although he took only tea. Adamu said, "I never respect this man, Mayode."

"So two cheers for Independence!—but give me four bottles of beer, will you? I have to take some to the Chief."

He walked out back to his patio, circled the house, and came back inside for the beer. He stood a moment, picked up the bottles, and told Adamu he was leaving. The cab of the kit-car gleamed in the sunlight; it was only nine months old. Britten had spent many hours prodding superiors and freeing up funds so that he could buy it. As he drove down the hill, he said aloud, "Hell, it's mine."

Chief Malen's compound was fronted by a bronze statue of indeterminate age and less-than-life-size stature. Behind the compound to one side lay the mosque, and to the other the weekly marketplace. The circular wall of the compound contained only a few squat interior buildings but the ornamental sculptings in the wall near the front as well as the structure's size reflected the chief's status. The *katamba*, or entrance hall, also held a rare double-panel door, in which were carved, after the local tradition, totemic animal figures and warriors' knives.

With a right derived less from long acquaintanceship than from prior notification of his arrival, Britten walked quietly through the entrance to the darkened inner *katamba* where the Chief conducted business. He peered in and tapped lightly on the door-jamb. "*Mi ga yida*—May I come in, sir?" He rubbed his palms on his shorts.

The Chief shifted his avoirdupois from his arm-chair and slowly straightened, supported by his wooden staff. "Oh yes," he responded in English. "Come in, Mr. Britten."

"*Kubetin.*" Britten's *Nupé* faltered as they shook hands limply. He presented his beer, and the Chief thanked him, in a way that showed he intended to speak English.

For Britten there was a second, wooden chair. The room was notable for a display of Bida-brass ceremonial ornaments but was otherwise devoid of furnishings except

110

for a raffia rug, several elaborately carved stools—each hewn, in the Nupé tradition, from a single tree trunk—and a table, on which sat a costly transistor radio. "Thank you for giving me some of your time."

"Not at all."

"And how are you today, sir?"

Chief Malen nodded in a fat, impassive way; his fez-like cap barely covered his balding head. "I am quite well."

"Very good, sir."

With great ease the chief said nothing, nor did he appear to have anything on his mind.

"I believe the Harmattan may be coming, sir," Britten remarked. "It's a bit cooler today."

"Yes, it's a bit cooler."

He cleared his throat. "Soon Jolima will have electricity. That will be a grand moment, won't it?"

"Oh yes, electricity." Chief Malen covered a yawn. "I am very excited for that."

"Of course. It's hardly the same town I came to nine years ago."

"Yes, there have been many changes."

"You were new to the chieftaincy then. I must say, much has happened during your reign and the people owe a great deal to you. It's really very difficult to believe you could do so much in that short span of time."

Chief Malen's eyes remained limpid. "We have worked hard, that is true."

111

Britten found his foot tapping drum-fire on the floor, too noisily for the little room, and crossed his legs. "I believe I've helped in some small way myself."

"You have helped." The chief nodded. "Oh indeed, you have done very well, as I have told you before. We are grateful."

"But after all, I consider Jolima my town too, you see." He switched to *Nupé*. Rubbing his palms and gazing hard at the concrete floor, he paused slightly before continuing. "It looks, Sir, as if they have sent that man—*a ga la ndannan byo*—to replace me."

"I see." The other man stared impassively out the doorway, fondling the leopard's-head crest of his staff.

"Well sir, I shall certainly give Mr. Alieu all the help he needs because of course I want the union to succeed"— he reverted to English because it was difficult to say in Nupe precisely what he wanted to say—"and though he seems rather to be bulling his way in, I know he'll work very hard to that purpose. But I should regret leaving after all these years; I had hoped to stay on even beyond normal retirement age." He stopped, and caught the chief's eye an instant before the chief averted his gaze.

"Yes, we should be sorry to lose you."

"You know sir, this is still one of the very few unions showing a profit—or to have its own vehicle—and there's no doubt that I can improve the record if I'm given more time." He risked a statement of belonging, stumbling slightly. "I—*ze Nupé*—I'm almost like one of your people." He thought of Mary reacting to his statement.

A smile came to the other man's lips—a slight smile physically but extensive in its implications. The Chief replied, "Yes, we feel you belong to us."

"I can't use *Nupé* back home—but why call it 'home'? This is my home now. A few weeks once every tour, that's enough of England for me. Frankly it's more than enough." He laughed sharply. "I no longer care for winters."

The chief nodded somberly.

"For your information, I'm more than a year and a half from 55. And I enjoy my work." Britten wet his lips. "It makes a chap feel old, you see. *N'wa ke degi*," he concluded. "Just a little longer."

"Well, I have decided to call on Mr. Mayode," the chief blurted. "I intend going to the capital tomorrow."

"Very good." Britten leaned back in his chair and pulled out his handkerchief to wipe his forehead. "I knew I should have your support."

"Yes, we shall see."

"*Kubetin,* sir." Britten fell silent, waiting for the chief to dismiss him.

Returning home from Kaduna with his son, Chief Malen felt modestly satisfied. He had not relished the long drive to the northern capital, nor dealing with a permanent secretary who offered him only a token show of respect. But in truth, times were not easy in Jolima, either, where he was caught between the new Northerner Alieu and the expatriate Britten. He could not speak directly of these matters to most of his subjects, but on the way back, when he had accomplished what needed to be done, he spoke in a way that he hoped his son Foday would understand.

"Never let them interfere," he began. He rode alone in the back seat of the big Mercedes; Foday sat in front with the driver. "They were mere clerks, but when a clerk sits in the office of a big man like Mayode, he begins to think he can just push you this way and that. *Wu a gaga*. But you are only a chief when you act like a chief-—never forget that."

The Chief used English when he didn't want the driver to understand him. Foday, with years of schooling behind him, spoke English comfortably. Sometimes the Chief believed his oldest son was becoming too Western, but it was clear that Foday appreciated the benefits of traditional power and his newly-conferred status of *shaba*, the heir apparent. "These hot-headed young nationalists may speak of us disdainfully, but they need us," he continued. "At least they know in Mayode's office that I must be shown respect,and I want you to act the same way when your time comes."

Foday nodded, his eyes on the odometer. Dauda, the driver, was paying little attention to his speed.

"You saw what I did. When they say to you 'Please sit,' 'Please wait,' you just remain standing and hold the staff so that they realize your time is not to be trifled with. Then they must take you into him or you shall make every one uncomfortable. Is he a permanent secretary, is he a minister, is he a governor or the chief of state? It doesn't matter, you see." He leaned back and fondled the crest of his staff.

"But Mayode—well, he considers himself as important as any *gitsu*. I do not say that he can be handled without tact; he has his own special authority and you will want the help of people like this. I am careful with all these bull-headed nationalists. Even that Kanuri man Alieu. You know of course that I went to Mayode because of him? Yes. You will be surprised to learn that he speaks no *Nupé*—not a word, so far as I know. Am I to communicate with my own cooperatives officer in another tongue?"

They left the tarmac and began to bounce along on the bumpy laterite road. Since Dauda still hadn't slowed down, Malen spoke sharply to him.

"The expatriate, Britten, also came to me about it," he went on. "If Mayode and his ilk have their way you will never have to deal with men like him. I don't say that you should; I only ask, what is the hurry that has come into our country since independence? You see, expatriates threaten them—Mayode and his puppet, Alieu—but not me. I am quite prepared to make use of them as I have always done, even as my father did, though they didn't know they were being used. Our Britten is a peculiar, jumpy fellow, but he has helped me and never meddled. On the other hand I do not trust this Alieu. Do you think he would willingly haul my groundnuts to market in the union lorry?"

He preened as he looked at his new 20-jewel watch. It was already 5:30, and the watch tended to run slow; they would be very late returning.

He said to Foday, "Well, I can't say things are as good as they used to be. These new men want to change everything—*wuruwuru*—and they are disrespectful to those who are senior to them and better. When I was a boy your grandfather was known across the land. What power he had! They feared him, you know. Some one couldn't come among our people against the wishes of the *Gitsu*.

"But today, a man like Alieu can walk into my compound and say he wants to see me, like that! And he simply informs me that he has been sent to work in my chiefdom. Perhaps he expected me to be grateful that he paid his respects. But that is of course a custom to be observed as long as there are chiefs, and you must never be careless with it. Inside Jolima, every stranger must recognize you or he shall not stay."

Foday seemed to be dozing. Chief Malen roused him.

"But when you are outside our chiefdom," he said after a moment, "you must proceed very cautiously in these times. You must calculate what it is you want most, and how much you are willing to give for it." They came to the river, with the ferry just approaching. Foday got out to tell the drivers ahead of them to move aside; the chief and he were soon crossing the stream. Foday stood beside the car until they reached the other side.

The chief settled his robes. "As I went into that office today," he said, "I estimated how much I could expect from Mayode, though I do not like to think this way when I am dealing with a man who has no chief's blood in him. But I knew what I could expect from the minister, and I thought of the Governor, though even from kinsmen you can now expect only so much. As I say, I remembered all that as I walked in.

"Oh, he observed the courtesies, he had his kola nut to break with me and he tried to greet me properly but I could see he was in a hurry. As soon as I mentioned Alieu he asked, 'How is the man settling in?' and I thought he seemed amused. So I spoke again of the man's sudden arrival and up goes the telephone, he calls for the files on Alieu and Britten and down goes the phone again, bang. He is so violent. Believe me, I would rather deal with an expatriate or any other stranger. Even when he bites into the kola nut it sounds as though his teeth are breaking, and once he jumped up and ran to the window to empty his nose. It was like thunder! And we are not in Ramadan yet. I mention this only to show you the personality of these new men. But probably you have observed this yourself."

"Yes Sir," Foday said. "Thank you, Sir."

"Very well, then, how do I deal with them? I would do it somewhat differently next time. I wasn't prepared for Mayode making immediate decisions irrespective of my wishes. Impatience, that's it; they have no time. 'We must not continue to rely on these expatriates,' he said. It seemed that whenever I spoke of Alieu, he answered about Britten. 'The man would reach retirement age before the end of his next tour,' he said.

"But you see, I knew all that. Britten had informed me that he was fifty such-and-such; he said would stay on several more years if he could."

"*U de wala*," Foday commented.

"Yes, his hand is unlucky. He certainly wanted the one tour he still had coming to him, and in Jolima. Much of this he said in *Nupé*. Did I tell you he brought me four bottles of beer? Of course he had come a few times before without this *emisa*, but I have no reason to complain of Britten. If he too is in a hurry, he has at least learned that I observe proper customs and don't rush."

Foday had turned on the radio. They stopped talking to listen to the music for a time and the Chief fell asleep. When he woke it was dusk, yet they were still twenty miles from Jolima. He asked Foday if his son had understood everything they had discussed, or wanted him to continue.

"I understand," Foday said. "Your wisdom has been very helpful. You needn't tire yourself further."

"Some day you will have to deal with these hurry-hurry fellows," the Chief continued, "and you should know that the less power you have, the harder you must work to keep your people's respect and your own self-respect. The mistake I might have made today—I drew back in time but it was a mistake to treat a permanent secretary as an equal.

I let his reputation as the dominant force mislead me. For civil servants a chief should have no time. So when he said 'Alieu is settled in now, there is nothing I can do,' I told him he was wasting my time and I should see the minister. A mans who says *u djin kamata* is not fit company for a paramount chief, do you see? When you are a chief you don't know those words, even if you are poor and have only 15 people to support you. Here on this staff is my symbol, the leopard's head. The Paramount Chief of Jolima is strong and terrible.

"So I said, 'Take me to the minister' and when you are chief you should speak just so. Always make them realize they need your good will, and that nothing goes for nothing. So now I have a letter for you to deliver to this man, Alieu. Of course I did not get complete satisfaction, and you must be prepared to pay a price, but never, never pay with your own dignity. You draw lines—so and so and so—around your power and keep it hidden from view, even if everything outside it must be sacrificed. The bull-headed ones ride high now, and you must understand their power without recognizing it. But the way they must view us is precisely the reverse—do you see that?

"Foday?" He leaned forward. "*Ci mi le*! It is just the opposite with them. Do you see?"

Foday turned and stared at him—then dropped his eyes. "I do see," he said.

Yes, thought the chief, there is hope for the paramount chieftaincy.

When Adamu brought his beer Britten said, "You're sure the Chief came back last night?"

"So them be telling me. And the van is there, by his compound."

"He's tired, I suppose." Britten tried to stop his foot, which had become a blur of motion. "And can't be bothered to hurry. But could he have sent a messenger while we were both out?"

"Well—I don't think."

"He'd send to the office—quite right. That's where I'd best be getting to." He set down his bottle and walked out to the kit-car, stumbling once. For a moment, he stood looking out over the valley and hills behind the house; then he started up the small van and drove down into the town. But when he walked into the office, Alieu was not there. He looked at Yaya.

"Where is he? Off to his prayers?"

"I think he has gone to visit the Chief."

He straightened. "Chief Malen?"

"Yes sir. The Chief sent for him."

"I see." Britten turned toward the door, then completed the circle. "Did he send for Mahmoud or for me?"

"For Mr. Alieu," Yaya said, his eyes wide.

Britten went to the window behind his desk, where by craning his neck he could see the Chief's compound. It was growing hot, and no one seemed to be moving in the streets. Yaya and Karimu were watching him; he seated himself. He nodded to them and said, "Things will have to go rather differently now, you know. Mr. Alieu is strict."

"Very strict," Yaya said, and Karimu grinned. "Of course, I don't know why—"

"Hmm?"

"I don't know why they brought this new man here."

Britten turned away. His eyes fell to the papers on his desk, and his fingers fluttered among them. Once he walked to the window but he didn't stop to stare out; he stretched his arms and seated himself again.

It was nearly one before Alieu came walking up briskly. His jaw was set.

"Well," Britten said, "I gather you've been to see the Chief."

Alieu took his seat and began an inspection of the files, in his composed and dignified way. Britten wanted to shake him.

"How is Chief Malen today? Tired from his travels?"

"He did not seem so."

Britten ran his hand through his hair. "Mahmoud." When Alieu looked up he said, "Did he say anything about wanting me to look in?"

"No."

"I see." With a nod Britten went back to his work, sorting through the papers and separating them into piles. As the heat mounted, the small office became oppressive. Alieu seemed not to notice but turned over the pages of a ledger at regular intervals. Yaya shifted in his chair. Karimu slipped out for a few minutes and returned still chewing on his meal. Gazing at the ceiling, Britten tapped a pencil on his thumb. Perspiration trickled out of his sideburns, and he wet his lips.

He met Yaya's gaze and got to his feet. "I'm going to visit the Mara society," he said. "You seem to know what you're doing, Mahmoud, so just muck in. I won't be back this afternoon of course."

Alieu looked at him. "Tomorrow morning I will want to use our van."

"I see."

Yaya pulled a blue folder from the file rack. "Will you be needing the Mara file, Sir?"

"Yes. Very well." He took the file, walked out to his kit-car and started the engine. After listening to it briefly, and staring at the office, he put the van in gear and drove into the town slowly.

It was very hot; no one was on the streets. The club would be closed at this time. Hawkins would be working. He could see Foday Malen smoking outside the chief's compound but decided not to speak to him. He wondered where to go.

Mahmoud Alieu's thoughts on the next morning came in this order as he heard the van's engine roar and rose from his prayer:

A man can't even pray.

Shirin is pretty but when next I transfer which despite Mayode will happen soon I must take Habiba. She will be vexed with me now and Shirin will have to suffer too for being the favorite but she must learn how to make mutton stew. The senior wife sees one through changes and transfers and I must send for Habiba tomorrow.

My stomach feels as though it's full of stones

—though it might be that officious letter and not Shirin and possibly everything else about this exile the man has imposed. How long? Two years, three?

"Continue the policy already established." Mayode thinks he's a modern man with his telephone and calculator and clerks with typewriters, but he will not survive the next revolution.

An apology to that reactionary! Malen and his sort ought to be deported too. Let him watch—I'll fire Karimu, make the others earn their pay and show them the old ways are at last dying, five years after the funeral.

The man talks too much and may not even know yet, and there will be this sulking, this distraction in the office. Perhaps I should feel sorry for him.

It's no use now trying to sleep.

He doesn't even have a woman; what keeps him here among strangers? So much beer, phew. Somehow he has succeeded and I know the attitude, "It will all go smash without me."

But I will manage, too—Mr. Permanent Secretary will have to take notice. I will eliminate the waste, yet if

Malen persists in humoring these chiefs with their heads in the sand! I must "continue the policy already established" but see if any of these other colonial puppets gets his goods hauled as though we were slaves.

This is not the 1940's, it's 1965. He wants me to fail, he doesn't think I hear *Nupé*. None of them knows yet. And if I don't understand, Habiba does—another reason to bring her. Mayode will like anything which hems me in but he'll find I can't be sent to bush and forgotten.

If I had called Shirin to me this morning, I would have forgotten this stomach and would not be tired and irksome.

He's coming this way too fast, too fast—he'll hit one of those laterite heaps before we get him out of here. It is natural to return home; why should he resist?

Listen to that van shudder; he's bumping over the edge of those heaps. Stop it! You'll wreck my van.

THIS IS KANO

(Reprinted from *Antietam Review,* XXIII (2003), 17-23)

Mohamed didn't understand North from South. One of the traders and other men were talking, of Northern Nigeria dwarfing the southern provinces of the country. He heard them say that Kano was the largest city of the north. He remembered that it terrified him when he walked through one of its gates, but now it was home. The Kano emir, they said, was one of the most powerful in Usman dan Fodio's old Hausa-Fulani empire. Men interrupted his sleep with talk of the Emir and the Imam and the Mutawali and the other Muslim officials. All he knew was that he had slept in the Kurmi market for many rainy seasons and that because of his face he might beg for coins, so most days he could feed himself. Also, that he must never see his father again. He tried to shut out the voices.

Now the sun rose again over the Mutawali's house, boring into Mohamed's eyes. Rolling over, he escaped it and slept until its heat sent a hot puff out of his tattered riga and onto his chin. An Igbo or some other Southerner stepped on him and cursed him. He rose to one elbow; when he tired of that he lay back again; later he sat up. The flies swarmed around him. Nearby, the trader he knew best was folding and arranging the cloths in his stall: selling, folding, saying his prayers, and rearranging. Small overloaded buses went by a few steps away in the littered street, their horns warning the crowd that a body in the way would be struck down. A goat ate the orange peelings near his feet. He napped, then sat up when the heat and his hunger forced him awake.

"Gimme dash," he begged of a woman walking by with a tray of groundnuts on her head. She looked at his face but passed on without giving him a coin.

A man with a stack of cloth on his head stopped to stare, another new person. "Gimme dash," he said but it was no use. The man pointed at him and laughed. "Hole-in-Face," he cried.

He got up and hobbled into the interior of the market, where there were piles of rice and yams and guinea corn and peppers and onions and meat and cakes. He saw one of the butchers drop a piece of intestine in the dust and accidentally step on it. He hobbled up calling. When the butcher saw what Mohamed wanted, he picked up the intestine and threw it at his feet. Mohamed scooped it up and ate it. Once when he was walking on the road that took him to Kano, he had eaten only *tsaidau*—weeds and earth. Back then, he was a boy fleeing his town, Wudil, and his father, and that day the road led through empty, sandy spaces. He passed through two or three villages, but Dawaki Kudu came in the middle of the day, when it was so hot that not a single person walked outside his compound. There were no good Muslims to give him alms. People looked away from him. Someone complained about his smell; that was the first time he knew that others smelled him too. He was shit.

The trader who always gave him a wheat-cake—see him, he told himself. He found the man, and when he had eaten the cake his stomach felt good. He lay down beside a potter's shed, but two small boys kicked dirt on him to force him away. A few stalls down was a man from Wudil who sold daggers. "Gimme dash," he said. The man gave him a penny from a matchbox and told him to go away.

He limped to the edge of the market, crawled into a box, and fell asleep. He saw his father in his sleep, and it was not good. When he woke the sun had begun to soften on the tin roofs of the market stalls. The tailors were finishing their day's work and walking off together, their machines on their heads. He plucked at their clothes and asked them to give him money, but they ignored him or laughed at his face.

He remembered himself as a child, before he had the hole. His mother could not feel things with her hands. She and Mohamed worked in the market, selling the pots that his father paid people to make. But she could not handle the pots carefully. Once while his father was present, she dropped a big water jar and broke it. His father screamed at her. Mohamed stood very still, looking at the ground. His father hit her; she cried out and he hit her again. Mohamed stared at the ground.

Later, when they knew she had leprosy, his father dismissed her as "the kutare," while his new young wife smiled. His mother grew clumsy in her cooking. Because she could not feel the fire in her fingers, she burned them off. His father beat her. He said he would send her back to her family and Mohamed too and demand his bride-wealth back. Mohamed was the only child he had with her. But her family was too poor even to support a sick woman. There was no chance they could repay the bride-wealth.

His mother continued to cook, but without her fingers she was clumsy. Food was dropped and his father said that the spillings of tuwo porridge would be all that she and Mohamed could eat. Finally he sent her back to her family. Then Mohamed developed spots and lost feeling in his face. His father grew angry and beat him. When he knocked off Mohamed's nose, he said Mohamed was a piece of shit and would have to go to his mother's family. But Mohamed's mother told him he couldn't stay in her family's compound. She gave him a coin she had hidden and said he should go to a big town where there were imams and good Muslims who would feed him. Mohamed bought food and began walking.

No one would take him. No one would touch him; he learned that he was untouchable. Good Muslims gave him pennies, but most people turned away or rebuked him for smelling bad. He walked and walked and walked; he reached Kano. There was a quarter for the kutare, but he knew none of the other lepers, and there was no food. The maigida there called his people "the Dead." Mohamed stayed in the market. He begged. Once a townsman informed him that his mother had died.

He noticed a stream of millet flowing from a hole in a sack astride a donkey; a goat wandered over to nibble on the grain. He kicked the goat aside with his good leg and scuffed it up. Yet his stomach wanted more, and the goat was pushing at him and still eating the grain.

The man who made sandals from old tires was saying his prayers. When he had finished, Mohamed got a penny from him; the man had many coins in his purse. He heard another beggar cry out that the Imam was coming, and he hurried to the dusty street. Alongside the others he said a loud prayer and saluted the Imam and like them received a penny. The Imam wouldn't touch him, but he dropped the penny in Mohamed's hand.

He felt peace. He put two pennies in his armpit, where he could feel them, and hobbled back to the cloth trader, who kept extra fura in his bowl. "Food,' he said. The cloth trader wore a good riga that kept him warm and dry when the rains came.

The man filled a small tin dish and held it out to him, keeping a thumb hooked over the edge. Mohamed offered him the penny in his hand. "Two pennies," said the trader. When he shook his head the trader poured half the pap back into his own bowl. Mohamed fretted, shaking his hands, but the trader laughed at him and again offered the half-portion. When he drew out another penny, the man refilled the dish.

He stuffed the food down his throat with both hands. He felt good, good. There was a sheet of newspaper lying in the street, which he rescued and spread on the reeking earth. As he lay down, the Mutawali's big house across the street turned a reddish brown; the dust and the children took on the sunset colors. The heat lingered as the sky grew gray, and the mosquitoes whirred by his ear. The groundnut vendors brought out their lanterns, which pockmarked the sleepy evening.

He closed his eyes but soon, restless, eased himself up to go in search of Mata the beggar woman. When he got to the area where she slept, he made noises for her, and she answered. There was another woman with her whom he had seen: she had her fingers and her nose even though her face and hands were covered with gray spots; that was the way he looked when his father started beating him. He didn't fear women. He needed them. He told this woman to open her cloth, but she asked Mata who it was and laughed when Mata said "Hole-in-Face." He remembered: he was nothing. He felt for Mata, who said, "Penny." He grunted. She opened her cloth; he lifted his rag and mounted her; the other woman laughed. He gave Mata the last penny, walked back to his sleeping place, and lay down for the night.

Someone was prodding him. He felt it a long time before he lifted his head. There was daylight in his eyes, but he could see the round broad brims of two police caps silhouetted against the sky, and two sticks were hitting his arm. "Get up," one of the policemen said.

He whimpered, pretending to feel their sticks; they prodded him. "I'm coming," he said. The smaller man prodded him again as he hobbled to his feet.

"Let's go,' said the big policeman. They pulled him hard by the sleeves of his riga.

"Phew!" said the other.

"Eh, leave him. It's not his doing."

"But why this week? They knew I wanted my holiday. You know she was going to meet me." The policeman looked Fulani and spoke the Hausa of the far north—one of the proud ones.

"She'll be there tomorrow night. And the roundup takes a lot of hours."

"Move!" the smaller policeman yelled as Mohamed held back.

One on each side they dragged him out of the market with their clubs in the sides of his back. He was afraid and resisted, but they pushed him. The daylight moved, and they saw Worm-Eye. The big policeman said, "You take this one. I'll bring the other."

"I won't touch him."

"That's understood. What? Are there no lepers in Katsina?"

Mohamed thought, "I am untouchable." He was pushed down the street by the smaller man, who was strong and who did not care about his leg. It was only his leg that hurt. When he whimpered the man prodded him, but that didn't hurt. "Go," the man said. "I warn you not to cause me any trouble."

He was afraid of the man. The police had rounded up the beggars before, but there was less hitting that time. And he had escaped because no one watched him the way this one did.

There were other policemen, all of them pulling beggars in the same direction. His leg hurt. They reached the policemen's place, where he was shoved onto a bench underneath a juju, the magic that made daylight at the side of the house, beside the other beggars—Hole-in-Leg, No Fingers, and Heavy Foot. They didn't speak with him, but they knew him: he was Hole-in-Face.

Mata and the beggar women were seated on the ground by the compound wall, and the small beggar boys stood quietly by the lorry shed. The bench and the standing space were filled as more policemen came with more beggars. It was not warm now; he shivered. The big man began asking questions of the beggars on the near end of the bench; the hard, small one stared at Mohamed, who was afraid. That man seemed dangerous.

Mohamed tried to sleep, but he was frightened, and then that man punched him on the arm with his club. He looked up, whimpering..

The big policeman said, "What is your name?" The policemen all had shiny things on their caps and on their shoulders and on the black things they wore around their stomachs. All had the secrets of light and Mohamed thought they must be jujus with frightening powers. The big policeman was the Mai, the chief of the station, and powerful. Powerful.

"Hole-in-Face," Mohamed whimpered.

"Shit!" said the hard man. "Your real name, quickly."

"Mohamed Maza."

They didn't hear him right, and he repeated his name while that man prodded him with his club.

"Why were you sleeping in the market?" the big man said. "Stop this foolish crying. We've brought you in before."

"I'm a night watchman."

The hard one laughed. "What building do you watch?"

"The Mutawali's house."

"Not so. You were sleeping across the street."

"I also watch a trader's stall," he whimpered.

"You are lying. And you stink."

"Easy," said the big man. "Remember, this is Kano." He said to Mohamed. "You don't have to be frightened. We are going to help you if you behave properly. Now tell us the name of your village."

"Wudil."

The little man made marks on a book. "Your brothers are there?"

"No."

"Where are they then?"

He shrugged.

"Put down Wudil," the big man said. "There is no need to ask him any more questions. Take him with the others on the lorry."

"No Wudil!" His father lived in Wudil. His mother was dead. They were rounding up the beggars to send them away. He looked for a way to escape, but there were too many policemen.

The small man hit him on the shoulder with his club. "You are not going to Wudil yet, fool."

"The doctors will be looking at him," the big policeman said. 'Don't bruise him. Just put him on the lorry."

"It is beneath me to deal with this man."

"It is not," said the Mai. "You may be a prince in Katsina, but here you are one of my policemen."

The small man called two other policemen who pushed Mohamed to the lorry with their clubs. No-Nose and Worm-Eye and many others were in the lorry, and they were afraid. Some of them were crying. After he found a place to sit he was able to doze, but he woke when the motor rumbled with its fearful growl. He got used to the movement, except that it was cold in the back of the lorry.

After a long journey they stopped. He smelled hot food and the others did too. It was tuwo, cooked and hot. He clawed his way to the edge of the truck; he was going to find the food and eat it, but as he was about to drop to the ground some one hit him with a crutch and knocked him down, hard, so that he cried out. The others jumped on him before running for a building with daylight nearby. Finally he could get up; he hobbled after them, watching the policemen hit them with clubs. "You will all get food, the hard man shouted. "Get back."

Through a hole in the side of the building they saw a man pass out two pans of rice, which were placed on a table, and they pushed again, but again they were beaten back. The policemen let two beggars past; one was Worm-Eye, who tried to grab both pans. The other beggar struck him and the tuwo went on the ground, where they scratched for it, cursing each other. The hard man kicked them each in turn. "See how these fools behave," he cried at the unseen being inside. "You must put only one pan out at a time"

The arm emerged with another pan of tuwo, and they let No-Nose through. Mohamed shouted with the others and tore at them to be next. The policemen beat them harder than before, and that man stepped toward Mohamed with his club drawn over his shoulder; Mohamed shrank back. Another beggar was permitted to pass. No-Nose reached for his pan and had to be knocked down. Mohamed tried to push between the two men in front of him, but he was hit on the head by the hard policeman, who moved quickly. "I'm glad my woman can't see this one because she might leave me," the man called to the other policemen, who laughed.

Mohamed whimpered, afraid. His head felt strange; he fretted about, wanting to get nearer the table. Someone grabbed his arm and pushed him forward. "Go on, then," the man said. Mohamed couldn't feel it, but he was sure that man had touched him. Yet he was untouchable.

He seized his pan of millet and looked each way to be sure no one would snatch it from him; the policemen laughed. He looked, unbelieving, at the rich food. There was a spoon in the pan, but he crammed the tuwo into his mouth with his hand. It had pepper. It was good, it was good but it was finished too soon, and when he looked at the hole that hard man pushed him away with his club. "You've had your share," he said.

He watched the man. Policemen didn't like him. They carried sticks and wore strange clothes, like Southerners and devils. Their rigas covered only the tops or their arms, and they had no clothes for the bottoms of their legs except their strange sandals. Then there were those terrible shiny jujus they carried on their chests and waists like little Muslim amulets but with much greater power.

The policemen prodded him and the others who had finished through the door at the far end of the building. They were shown a strange place with big white holes, and how to use it, then taken into a long room full of more things he didn't know the names of, with blankets on them. He was told to sit on one; it was long and soft; each of the beggars had one. But he wanted to sleep, and when the policemen left he pulled off the blanket and went to sleep in the place between two of the things. He felt warm, but something seemed wrong with his head, and he was afraid.

The sun will still dull when that man, that Katsina Fulani, came, prodding him awake. "What is wrong with you?" he said. "Don't you know that a cot is to sleep on?"

He was frightened.

"Don't alarm him" said a new voice.

He sat up, his arms sore, and looked at the two new men, who wore strange white rigas; one of the men was very light-skinned, a bature who averted his eyes and spoke to the other in the European language. They bent close to his face.

"Oh," said that man—the hard policeman—who turned away.

"Have you seen a doctor before about this?" said the one who spoke Hausa. "You should not be afraid. Just answer my question."

Mohamed shook his head, not sure he understood the man.

"He does not cooperate," that hard man said. "He just stinks and sits around taking up space."

"How many rainy seasons have you been this way?"

He shrugged.

"Many or not many?"

"Many."

The two men in white rigas spoke together. One looked at Mohamed's ankle and they talked again, talked and talked. The one who spoke Hausa said "Tau, madala"—they were done with talking. "This medicine is called Dapsone. It is very powerful and it will not hurt. Take it with this water—yes, now—then you can go back to sleep. We are going to keep you here a while longer." After the bature said something foreign to him, he continued, "It's all right. You are safe. We are going to give you more of this medicine so that you will not lose your fingers."

He shrugged, alarmed. Looking about him he found that many of the beggars were gone, and it was not good. Hole-in-Leg and he looked at each other without speaking. But when a boy brought him a pan of tuwo just as his stomach was beginning to hurt, he felt peaceful and good, good.

While he was eating, Walk-on-Knees began to laugh. He was holding a small, shiny thing and looking at it. He showed it to Worm-Eye, who looked at it and laughed. Worm-Eye wanted to hold it, but Walk-on-Knees pulled it away, pointed at Worm-Eye and laughed loudly.

Worm-Eye said, "Show it to Hole-in-Face." They shouted with laughter.

Walk-on-Knees crawled over with the thing and told him to look into it. Mohamed saw a strange face that moved when he did. "That's you!" Walk-on-Knees shouted.

Mohamed looked again; yes, there was a big hole. His face was different from others', and better for pennies in the market.

Walk-on-Knees laughed hard.   Mohamed also laughed at the strange face.   He tried to hold the thing where he saw the face, but Walk-on-Knees pulled it away and hit him and crawled back to his own bed, where he laughed and laughed at Mohamed, and the other beggars laughed and laughed, laughed and laughed.   Mohamed forgot about them and rubbed his leg where it hurt.

He sat on the floor, looking ahead of him at the bars in the window.   After a while he got up and slumped onto the cot.   It was soft; he was frightened when it seemed to sink under him, but he found that it was warm and good. He was ready to fall asleep, but they brought him rice, which made him feel peaceful.   It was good, because no one tried to take it from him.   But when he went to the place with all the white holes, he saw that that man was sitting in a room across from it.

When he woke next time every one was gone but Hole-in-Leg.   The men in the white rigas were talking to Hole-in-leg.   He could hear the Hausa man say Hole-in-Leg was being sent back to his village, that there was a place there where Hole-in-Leg must go for help.   The man pulled out something long and sharp and stuck it in Hole-in-Leg's arm.   Why he cried out, Mohamed didn't know.   Mohamed felt no pain in his arm, like true kutare.   Afterward policemen took Hole-in Leg away, and the two men in white rigas came over to Mohamed. They were all alone in the room. He was frightened; he fretted and whimpered.

"Be still," said the one who spoke Hausa. "I'm not going to hurt you."

He watched the man. The two men talked, and he heard those big foreign words—"leprosy" and "Dapsone."

"You are fortunate," the man said. "We are going to give you treatment for your disease before you go to—go away.

Mohamed's hands began shaking. The bature spoke to the one who knew Hausa.

"Oh, it will be very good treatment. If you take the medicine, you will not get any sicker."

He looked at the man, afraid. "Gimme food," he said, although he was not hungry.

"You will have plenty to eat. Just stay here tonight and take your food and tomorrow"—he waited while the other man spoke to him—"you will go to hospital for treatment."

"No, bring food." They weren't going to let him go. "Gimme dash."

"My friend wants you to understand. He wonders why you are so frightened. You do realize we are going to help you?"

"Bring food," he whimpered. They were going to keep him.

The two men talked again. Then the Hausa man said, "My foreign friend hopes you are pleased. You do understand, don't you?"

Mohamed fretted and mumbled to himself; the men were looking at him. They spoke to each other, turned away, and left the building.

A small boy came with two puff-cakes and a cup of tea. That man came out and told the boy to put the food on the floor. The boy did so and hurried away.

"There, stoop down for it," that man said. He hissed through his teeth. "Another night lost to your ugliness and your stench. You are shit, you know—why do you allow yourself to exist? They say they can help you, but they can't. There is no cure for the kutare, so why do they waste their time?' He breathed hard though his nose and walked away. My father spoke so, Mohamed thought.

There was no one else nearby. Mohamed was afraid. Nothing happened. He gazed at the window bars and thought about being free. There were no women here; he wanted a woman, but they wouldn't let him go.

He went to the strange place but was frightened by the rushing water, and by that man in his room. He didn't like to sleep here.

The daylight stopped. He crawled about his cot, not wanting to be alone in the dark with that man. They were going to spoil his face. He was afraid that man would hurt him.

When everything was quiet he got up, wrapped his blanket around himself, and picked up three blankets from another cot. It was hard to see, but he found his way to the door at the other end of the building. There was the strange place on one side and the little room on the other where he could hear the man sleeping. He pushed the door at the end, but it wouldn't open; he leaned against it, but a power held it. Then he found a hard thing on it which he pushed; it turned down and the door went open. He stepped to the ground, tripped on one of his blankets, and fell. His leg hurt.

"Hole-in-Face! What are you doing?" He didn't answer. "Get back in here or I will beat you."

He whimpered. "I am going to piss."

The man came to the door, his daylight with him. "Fool, that is why we have the latrine. Get back in here."

"But that place is noisy. There are devils there."

"Shut up." That man prodded him with his club and forced him to the strange place, the latrine. "I want no trouble from you. Instead of being with a new woman tonight, I am assigned to look at your face. Ea-ah! They are laughing at me right now. Oh yes, I am one of those proud Fulani-Hausa, and this is their lesson for me. Someone will pay. Get back to your bed."

Mohamed whimpered. He didn't like that man, who had powers even though he was not wearing his jujus now, only a riga But without his jujus he did not have power to see the blankets Mohamed was carrying.

144

"How do the women like your face?" that man laughed. "Do you have a girl in town—like me? Ha! Get to your bed. Now! Soon you will be out of Kano, and I won't have to smell you again."

Mohamed moved too slowly.

That man screamed. "I could kill you. Look, here is my pistol." He showed Mohamed a black, shiny juju. "No one would care because I am a policeman. And my ancestors came with Usman dan Fodio. But you are nothing!"

Mohamed returned to his bed and fretted, unable to sleep. There was pain in new places, and he knew that man was going to hurt him. He could hear him sleeping again. He picked up the blankets and walked softly trying to keep his bad leg from scraping the floor, to the entrance. That man was snoring. He opened the door and hobbled out. He couldn't move quickly, but he heard no sound behind him.

He didn't know where he was. He walked and walked, his leg hurting, his feet and head hurting, until he found a street he recognized. He didn't stop; he remembered how it was to walk and walk, and now he was afraid. He came to the great wall and walked around it until he found the gate by which he had entered the city many dry seasons ago. He knew where he was and he walked. Before he reached the market he grew tired, but he came to it and lay down across from the Mutawali's house, wrapping the blankets around him. His sleep was not sleep with his leg hurting him, hurting.

As the sun rose over the Mutawali's house he could feel a tug at the blankets and he stirred. The cloth trader had taken two. "Now, where have you been?" he said. "And where did you get these blankets? You stole them, didn't you?"

"Mine," he whimpered.

"Shall I turn you over to the police? No I shall keep two. Be thankful you have two left."

"Mine," he said, but the trader laughed and walked away.

He sat up. There were donkeys in the street. The sun was growing hot; he threw off the blankets and rubbed his sore places. The flies droned and buzzed over his face, then the Mutwali's children and grandchildren came swarming around to laugh at him, but they went away. Many bicycles went by; two collided. People looked at him, pointing their fingers and talking so he could not hear. I'm nothing, he thought.

The Mutawali's house turned lighter as the sun went higher, and the dust thickened over the market. There were no other beggars. The trader sold his cloth, prayed, sold, and rearranged. Mohamed slept, but it was not good. He saw his father pushing him away, no one feeding him. He remembered eating weeds and dirt along the road, that man beating him, people changing his face, that man cursing him, his father hitting his mother.

When his stomach felt empty, he got up, dragging his blankets in the dust, and went off to see the man who would give him a wheat-cake. Now it was peaceful inside him; his body hurt, but he wasn't afraid. The trader looked at him and looked all around the market before he handed over the wheat-cake. Mohamed ate it and settled down to sleep, and this time it was good, good. Then he woke.

Someone was prodding him.

THE BEAUTY QUEEN OF BONTHE

Thomas McCartney tucked his cassock between his large stomach and his heavy thighs, as he hovered over his gardenias and four o'clocks to caress them with a sprinkle from his watering can. It was his first task of the day and the least necessary. He could have turned it over to the household help, but he believed the public expected a priest to be a gentle man of nature; he perceived an approval of his tending flowers, as of his strolling by the river with his Bible or smiling on small children. Each morning at about seven, he was onstage in the little ton with his watering can. Passersby who peered at his large frame through the gate of the mission compound received cheerful, almost loving greetings, for this hour of the day found him at his most fatherly to the world in general. Later, small things might irritate him, although he didn't think he could be said to have a temper.

Sister Catherine was approaching along the street from the convent this morning, her head bobbing above the mission wall, and McCartney, seeing her out of the corner of his eye, hovered over his flowers. As she passed through the gate he looked up startled. "Why, good morning to you, Sister Catherine," he said. "What a pleasant surprise it is to see you so early in the day." He had known the Sister since his arrival in Sierra Leone 23 years ago, and had given up trying to like her.

"And good marnin' to you, Father," she said. "And you're watering your flowers again. It's a marvel, isn't it, that with all your care they never do well."

"This year, Sister," he said with a short chuckle, "this year they'll be grand. Just you wait and see." What a little dark cloud she was. Having come to the country seven years earlier than he, she tended to treat him like a junior brother.

"I'm afraid I've a piece of bad news," she said, rubbing her very white hands together. "Juliana was taken to the hospital last night and I've seen her this marnin'. She's quite ill."

"I thought she looked ill yesterday," he said, omniscient for the sister's benefit. "And what would the matter be?"

"A serious case of malaria, it seems. Dr. Turner is quite anxious about her."

"Well, 'tis sorry I am to hear it."

Sister Catherine shook her head. "It's a bit of a shock. Usually she's the picture of health, you know, so straight—yet round like a woman she is, now. And still that smooth brown complexion."

152

"Poor child. She's still a girl to me, you know."

"Well, Father, I must be going. I'll let you know what happens."

"Why," he said, smiling, "I'll be looking in on her meself. I take special interest in all me flock, you know." His mood improved as he saw her lips tighten. "I've an hour before school. I'll go now."

"Of course, it's possible you may not be admitted."

"We'll see, we'll see. Thank you Sister," he said, smiling broadly, "for bringing the news."

"And you're welcome, Father." She returned his smile as she serenely moved away.

He wondered why she told him. It was more like the nuns to conceal events at the convent or in the primary school. To them it was: let the Father run the secondary school and the mission and the parish as he wants, but not meddle in the Sisters' affairs. Now he was receiving medical bulletins on one of their teachers.

He walked toward the hospital, his cassock flouncing. He was fond of Juliana Darbah, a quick, wide-eyed girl who had virtually been raised by the Sisters, under his supervision, and as he strode along his fears rose. In his years in Sierra Leone he had encountered many young people with awful and incurable diseases, and buried more than a few.

Near the river he passed Manfred Erb's flat, where he hesitated before deciding he hadn't time to drop in. The little Canadian was seldom sociable at half-seven in the morning. He had layers, that laddie, secrets he revealed by trying so hard to conceal them. The Father turned right at the river, after a glance at his secondary school to the left on a bluff downstream, and entered the central wing of the long low hospital. From the maternity ward came the usual groans and cries, which at other times amused him; today he was preoccupied.

"Esther," he said to the buxom young nurse, "has Dr. Turner come in yet?"

"No," she said, looking away in her apathetic manner. "Oh yes, he is coming now."

"Good morning, Father."

Michael Turner had walked up behind him, quietly. Tall and light skinned, he had a narrow face and high-bridged nose that distinguished him from the Mende and Sherbro villagers. He nodded with customary distractedness to the Father's greetings.

"Michael, they tell me I've a sick girl under your care."

"Yes, Miss Darbah is here," Turner said quietly. "She is ill."

McCartney clucked. "Too bad. I hope you don't mind if I see her--?"

"Not at all. Perhaps she'll tell you something useful." He didn't smile.

"You're not sure about it, is that it?"

"I didn't say that." The doctor shook his head. "Oh, it's malaria—as she says."

"Oh, that. Well, let me talk with her."

Turner drew him toward a nearby room and asked him to wait outside until he had made his check. Without distinguishing the words, McCartney could hear his voice probing, apparently to no avail. He came out again. "I'll leave you alone with her," he said.

"Thank you, Michael."

McCartney was shocked when he stepped around the screen at the foot of Juliana's bed and saw the altered person who lay there. The girl's usually smooth and pretty face was haggard and sweaty, and she looked frightened. Yet she showed no interest in him.

"Well, Juliana," he said. "A bit sick? Yes 'tis sick you are indeed. But you're young, God be praised."

She looked away.

"What seems to be the trouble? Is it fever—?"

"Yes, Father," she whispered.

"Be sure you give Dr. Turner all the information he needs." There was no response. She had withdrawn behind an expressionless face. "Might it be something else? Maybe you ate something polluted?"

"I don't think." Less demure than most of the girls, Juliana when well had a brilliant smile, a minute of conversation for him, but today she was treating him like a stranger.

"Would you want to confess?"

Her eyes turned toward him and away quickly. "No, Father. I am not just well enough."

"I see." He looked out the window to the flamboyant trees along the riverbank and commented inconsequentially on the clear morning. She made no response. "God bless you," he said, irked. He made the sign of the Cross over her and left. Pushing through the mob of patients already pressing around the Doctor's examination room, he stuck his head in the door and told his friend that he had learned nothing new.

The doctor looked up politely. "It's a bit worrisome," he said. "I wouldn't expect her to respond so poorly to our care."

"All right, Michael. I'll be very interested in the developments." He closed the door and walked out of the hospital, smiling at the people he knew. Outside he found he had only fifteen minutes before school began and wished he had brought his bicycle.

He hurried toward the mission. How could Juliana be so sick and yet apparently indifferent? She was a proper girl. He had been proud of her for winning the beauty pageant last year—vain though such things of this world might be. Of course he found her pretty—she must nibble endlessly on her chewing stick to produce a smile like that—but why shouldn't a priest like a healthy well-formed girl? So long as she was virtuous, it was better she be pretty than plain. Surely she was chosen because she showed poise and wore a proper dress and because every one knew she was a girl of character; indeed she made the event respectable. Manny Erb might talk about the way her hips moved but Manny had an irreverent streak, the girl was good, and he was very concerned for her.

The wiry Canadian himself appeared, biking toward school. What was it he had said early on, with his mouth curled, about his foster mother's heft, and then realizing his mistake, backed away, fell silent, and revealed so much?

Erb's reluctant smile pushed back the borders of his dark beard. "Better hurry, Father. You'll miss the bell."

"Why, I'll be right behind you," McCartney responded. "I'm a powerful cycler, Manny, a powerful cycler, you know."

Scoffing, the younger man rode past. McCartney's spirits lifted slightly. He hadn't had time to tell Manny about Juliana but he would drop in after school for a beer, and they could talk it over. Manny was a good listener as well as a fount of energy who captivated his students. A pity he was leaving at term's end.

Having handled his flow of out-patients by noon, Turner managed an hour's rest after lunch, but couldn't relax with the Darbah case on his mind. Something unusual was afoot and he had no one to consult with. The girl did have malaria—he'd treated hundreds of malaria victims—but something more. It couldn't be hepatitis; there was too much pain and no appropriate symptom except anemia, which could mean many other things. The pain was in her lower abdomen but wasn't appendicitis. And then there was a smell about her. He had discussed the case with his wife through his lunch break and briefly with Massaquoi, the nurse on duty, who scarcely bothered to listen. He was glad to see Mrs. Kambara come on at 3:00. She asked first thing about Darbah.

"We're dealing with something complicated," he said. "Beyond fever."

She nodded, unsurprised. "It's very strange that she can't tell."

Turner watched her. Although less well-trained than the two younger nurses, Kambara was wiser, more compassionate, and humbler about her importance to the hospital.

"It could be some female trouble," she said.

If this were London, that would be the first response: she's got herself into some trouble with a man. But here attitudes were different. "She's hiding something, isn't she?" he replied.

"I want to think so. Perhaps she is embarrassed."

He shook his head. "She's an educated girl. Surely she wouldn't be prudish with me—?"

Kambara shrugged, but the gesture seemed not to mean that she didn't know.

"Why don't you talk with her again? You know women better"—he stopped—"I can really only deal with medical problems."

"Yes Doctor." She left him by the registration desk, and he immediately sat down. He was doctor to 8,000 people, director of the hospital, the public health official,

158

and the coroner for an entire chiefdom. Still, he believed that if he could hire another nurse or two like Kambara, he would manage. He wasn't too proud to want help—within limits: he would not admit to failing to make a diagnosis. Even McCartney, for all his Irish provincialism, might be helpful.

His head slumped to the desk but he raised it sharply, to avoid being seen half-asleep at the public entrance. He walked into his office, seated himself, and let his head sink again to his forearm. The girl complained only of malaria. Why couldn't she be more forthcoming? She was educated, responsible, usually open with her own. She should have been a good patient.

When an hour later Kambara wakened him with a soft call, he looked at his watch and remonstrated, "I have a handful of reports to make out." He went on, "Well, what about Darbah?"

"She doesn't tell me anything, Doctor."

"Do you think she's aware she may be seriously ill?"

"Yes. I told her. It's very strange though. I found her at the sink."

"She was able to stand?"

"She was leaning on it. She said she only wanted to see in the mirror if her face was looking better. She's vain, you know."

"What's happened to her?" He leaned back in his chair, thinking of X-ray apparatus long promised by ministry officials who had never been to his hospital or even Sherbro Island.

"Well, she's done something to herself, Doctor. I'm very sure of that." She wiped her hands on her uniform. "Now she's ashamed."

"She's holding her own health hostage, it seems. Maybe you can find out the reason, while I determine what's going on inside her. In any case, thank you. I'll look in on her later."

As the nurse stepped into the corridor he pulled a folder from his top drawer and began to write his reports. It was five by the time he finished and he still had his rounds to make. Fortunately, Darbah was his only serious case. When he checked on her he found her perspiring and writhing on her bed, but she made no complaint.

"You know," he said sternly, "you're a very sick girl, Miss Darbah, and you're mistaken not to give me a complete medical history. That is the way an illiterate woman behaves."

She made no reply. She had always struck him as insolent, but her silence implied something more. He took her temperature.

"Your temperature is much too high; it's nearly 40 degrees. If you don't want to suffer, you must tell me what has happened to you."

She murmured something but not, it seemed, to him.

"I see that despite your advantages, you remain trapped in the old ways."

Her soft brown eyes feigned indifference behind the thick lashes; her fingers twisted the sheet that covered her waist.

"Why did you come here, then?" He resorted to Krio: *"Wetin make you no go for juju doctah?"* She made no response. He had to move on. "Well, I shall leave you alone with your pain." After making sure she would remain silent, he left with simulated abruptness. He disliked her for making him feign annoyance.

Elsewhere in the hospital he found no one who needed his attention. He saw Kambara near the maternity ward and told her he was going home. "Give Darbah more aspirin and a sedative," he said. "She may be in considerable pain tonight."

She nodded, her white cap bobbing like a kite. "I was just thinking," she said, "about that girl. She has an auntie in town, you know."

"An auntie?" He pursed his lips. "Someone who can get her to talk?"

"Well—if you will permit it."

"Perhaps I will. Have her come in the morning."

"Yes, Doctor. Good night."

Turner peered briefly into the maternity ward and met the gaze of old Fatmata, a queer misshapen woman who believed she saw devils, and who walked around the town talking to them. Kambara told him it was the first time Fatmata had come to the hospital for delivery, though it was said that she had carried or miscarried several babies; he noticed that the other women generally avoided her. He counted 14 of them in the ward and hoped none would have a difficult delivery. He was thankful for Kambara, who could probably handle whatever came up while Mary Anne and he went out this evening. But of the 8,000 people in the chiefdom, probably 1,000 needed treatment of some kind. And if they were ever to overcome their old ways, they had to believe in him. He had to be good.

When the bell sounded to end classes, Erb walked to his bicycle, threw his hard bare leg over the seat and cycled down the hill. With only three weeks to go, he felt he was racing time. He pictured Lisa in Utrecht: was it worth going back to Holland? His thoughts drifted to Juliana Darbah and the perfect circles of her body, here in a remote coastal village of Sierra Leone, of all places.

Inside his flat, above the Lebanese store, it was close; the faded curtains lay listless against the verandah windows. He turned on the fan and put extra bottles of Star Beer in the fridge, for McCartney was coming by to tell him something about Juliana over a beer, and "a beer" with the Father implied any larger quantity. McCartney seemed to like him and had loaned him most of the furniture in the flat. It wouldn't be hard, physically, for him to pack up and go. Odd that the priest had once suggested that he, Erb, was overly interested in the things of this world. But maybe they had a sort of understanding.

He opened a can of carrot juice, made a beef sandwich, and seated himself in a soft chair. McCartney had been an interesting enough presence. For all the priest's jokes and pious poses he could give and take an epithet, and once had pummeled a thief he'd caught in his office. McCartney also gazed on the nubile girls who bathed at the riverside, a reassurance to Erb, whose previous contacts with the clergy had been rare and superficial. As for the Father's poses—well, better he should affect saintliness than display his short temper. He knew the hidden priest, having lived with McCartney and Father Clark, the district supervisor of Catholic primary schools, the first two months of his tour.

He finished his lunch. Before his thoughts could lead him back to Juliana he heard a clumping tread on the steps that he recognized as Fele's. She entered without knock or greeting, dropped into a chair in the corner, and resumed her vigil. He offered her a frown and leaned back in his chair with eyes closed. She came almost every day, a lumpy, unkempt old woman who claimed to be his wife. He sometimes had waking nightmares that she would demand connubial privileges. Once, after watching him work out, she had picked up one of his weights; another time, she opened the refrigerator and fingered food inside it. Mostly she just watched him from her chair, as impassive as the Bundu mask on the bookcase. By 3:45, when the Father arrived, his mind was elsewhere.

But McCartney noticed. He yammered at her in Mende until she fell back in her chair, overwhelmed and apathetic.

"So Lad," he said, accepting a beer: "You've taken old Fele as wife."

"She's taken me. It's been quite a romance."

"Did I ever tell you the time she did the same to Father Clark? She said she was the Father's woman, you know, and came hanging 'round the Mission. Wouldn't do, wouldn't do at all. Why Manny, people were gossiping about the two of them. So he finally removed her by force." He winked. "The Father has a nasty temper, you know."

Erb nodded. He had heard the story before. "You didn't make the bell this morning."

"Ah Manny, you've no sympathy for an old man." He took a long swallow. "Now why don't you let me tell you the news? Do you remember me saying that Juliana Darbah was sick?"

"Sister Catherine told me about her this morning. I thought she might be exaggerating."

"Ah, Sister Catherine told you, did she?" The Father winked again. "I'm afraid the Sister's a bit of a gossip."

"What's wrong with Juliana?" Erb pronounced her name carefully, as though to suppress the image of her body.

"Now there's the question. Michael won't tell me but I know it's no simple fever. Seriously, Manny, I'm worried about that girl. I was just at the hospital but Michael wasn't there. Ellie Kambara told me her condition was the same, and wouldn't say more, even though she likes to talk."

Erb nodded, waiting for more.

"You know how fond I am of her," McCartney continued, after a long drink. "She's first-rate, you know, first-rate."

"Yes."

McCartney held up his near-empty bottle to show he was preparing for the next. "Now I know what you've said about her, but believe me she has character. I've known her much longer than you—her entire life, in fact. Sure and she makes her mistakes and perhaps she doesn't confess often enough, but Manny Lad, this is a good girl, you know, a good girl."

Erb pulled another beer from the fridge. "You know I like to make your life difficult."

"You do, yes you do, Manny. But you have your redeeming qualities. You drink good beer and you can tell long stories without a word o' truth in them." He was the jovial Friar, winking, patting his large stomach and gulping from a fresh bottle. "Very important on quiet nights here in the bush, you know, to have some one who can entertain you with beer and blarney."

Erb wondered why the Father would say things so untrue. "I don't recall getting to talk that much."

"Faith, and what would you be implying? I remember you talking plenty when you were at the mission. Why, you told me about your days as a wrestler, and your travels here and there—I tell you Lad, I got an earful."

"I must have had too much beer, eh?"

"Now, you never drank that much." McCartney sighed. "But those were good times, Manny. We had our laughs. Well, we still do and I wish you'd stay on so we could have a few more. Now, don't bother to answer, I know I've no hope." He drank again; they both drank. "But I'm very troubled about this girl Juliana. Manny, I've known her all her 21 years and she's, well—she's a dear colleen, that's what she is."

"You're still worried about something I said last year, aren't you?" said Erb, sympathetic and annoyed. "Yes, I know exactly what's bothering you. If I'd realized what mischief I could create with little comments like that, I'd've had something to say about all your friends."

"Ah, you're a problem, my boy," the Father laughed, smoothing the perspiration from his thinning hair. "Bush does that to the most promising young fellows."

They could find no words for each other, and drank. McCartney looked ready for his next beer but said nothing.

"Doesn't your wife want a drink?" he finally asked.

"I've never offered."

Again McCartney spoke to Fele in Mende. Erb thought him too pleased with himself.

"Is she—?" he started to ask about Juliana.

"Oh no, you're quite right not to offer. You'd never be quit of her then."

"You?"

"No Lad. Thanks, I think I'll be going." He took his cord as if to pull himself up, then rolled forward to his feet—the pose of patriarchal infirmity. "I've a bit o' work ahead tonight."

Erb rose too. "But you've had only two beers," he said, straightening as the large priest stood over him. He was thinking how much McCartney wanted to befriend him, and how hard that made things.

"Well, it will be difficult but I'll manage, you know." Chuckling and winking McCartney backed toward the door. "I'll let you know about Juliana."

Erb closed the door behind the Father and sank into a chair. Juliana was wasted on a romantic Irish priest; only a McCartney, trying his best to equate beauty and virtue, could have missed it.

He rose and walked to his verandah, ignoring the brutal afternoon sun. Would the man give him no peace? It wasn't the first time he—or she—had broken up their conversation and made them both stare at the floor, rubbing their bottles. At other times the Father would sermonize on his vast knowledge of "the people," a lesson also pointed her way. Let him take long walks around the streets late of an evening, Erb thought, so that he might learn more about the town's private life.

Bad enough, Erb thought, that I've been forced to give up my own hopes. He stalked back to his parlor and seated himself. It's the closest I can come to love. After the years of searching and the parade of flawed women, here she was—as he was about to have another birthday and to move on again. She had been sacrificed on McCartney's altar.

He lunged to the floor for his calisthenics. Fele leaned forward to watch, curious. He bounced up again. "Come, come," he said. "Leave me to my own fantasies, will you?" Opening the door he motioned her out. She left, poker-faced, laconically tucking in the ends of her head-tie.

Turner realized, as about nine o'clock he strung his tie around his neck, that he was too tired for a party and should go to bed, but he needed something besides the Darbah case to think about, he owed the time to Mary Ann, and she craved diversion, inasmuch as she found the town small and dull. So he would go. They had hoped when they came out, fourteen months earlier, that she could teach at the secondary school, but Father McCartney wouldn't hire non-Catholic local staff. Turner tried not to remember that McCartney hired a non-Catholic Canadian, who wandered in for unknown reasons.

Mary Ann had spent a year in suspended animation—a waste, he felt, with her degree, with her impeccable English. She should have a child. Birth control was a hard secret to hold and there were already many things setting them off from their fellow Africans. Sooner or later she would drive him—he caught himself—they would have to move back to Freetown.

He heard her singing to a record in her pouty voice. Seeing her in his mind's eye he wanted her, and felt good about going out. But as he was ready to enter the front room he heard a knock and familiar voice at the door.

"But why? Can't it wait?" Mary Ann spoke English even with messengers. Deep down, she had her own unspoken educational mission, to bring culture to the bush. She rarely spoke Krio even with him.

Turner couldn't make out the messenger's response but he knew what was being said.

"Tell her he'll come by later. He has an engagement now."

Unwillingly he stepped out and met her disappointment. "My dear, Mrs. Kambara would never send for me unless it was an emergency. You know how she protects me."

She turned away, her full skirt swishing at her knees. "It always happens," she said.

He sent back word with the messenger that he was coming, while she stood motionless, looking delicate in her fitted blouse. "It can't be helped," he said.

"It's Juliana Darbah, I suppose. And you won't be able to do a thing for her."

"I must try. I hate losing young patients."

She turned away. "Mrs. Kambara is probably right. I know I've called her a bush woman but she does understand these things. It's woman trouble or man trouble, however you look at it. That Darbah creature has wiggled her hips once too often."

"Possibly not." What mattered in Darbah's case was not her nubility but her education, which she wasn't using. "Why don't you go to the party alone and let me try to make it later?"

"I don't want to go without you. I'd have to be so restrained."

He laughed. "You don't want Erb lifting you off your feet with his powerful dance moves?" When she grimaced, he said, "Consider it a tribute."

"Shouldn't you have been offended?" she countered. "Or even jealous?"

"I was simply puzzled. I scarcely know him but he seems to have hidden desires."

"Not so hidden."

"As you wish." He picked up his bag. "I must go. Perhaps I can finish in an hour or so."

"Try." She spoke sulkily, charming him.

He shut the door behind him, got into the car and drove the short distance along the river-front to the hospital. Kambara met him at the door, but what she had to say was unnecessary: he could hear Darbah 's cries. He would not be going home in an hour.

"She's been like this for about 45 minutes," the nurse reported. "But she still just asks for quinine and says it's fever. And she washes herself."

"Washes herself. She got up again? How do you know?"

"She climbed back in bed just as I came in. And the sponge was wet in the sink."

"Where is her temperature?"

"A small time ago it was 40 degrees. That's when I sent for you."

They entered her room and found her writhing eyes closed, suppressing her outcries. With Kambara's help—and without the apparently modest Darbah's—he stripped her soaking gown from her and searched her body for any bruise or laceration he might have missed before, indifferent in the presence of pain to her round nudity. He pressed above her abdomen.

"Any pain?"

The girl shook her head, eyes still closed. He wasn't surprised. But when he pressed at the base of her abdomen she placed her hand in his way.

"The worst of it is there, is it?"

She nodded. Aware of the smell between her legs, she pulled the sheet over her.

"Juliana," Kambara said in Mende, "you've done something to yourself and you've got to tell us what it is. What will your mother say? We'll be sending for her. And your auntie, oh my."

Juliana started and flicked her eyes open. "Tell us," Turner said in English, which came more easily to him. "I warn you, you're a very sick girl."

When she didn't answer he eased her onto her side and inspected the soft brown back. There was nothing to see but classically healthy youth.

"She'd better have a clean gown," he said. Mrs. Kambara brought one from the closet. With a sudden burst of energy, Darbah seized it and pulled it on without lifting the sheet.

A new reading showed her temperature had not changed. She was crying out again.

"Give her more aspirin." The ministry's consignment of morphine was a week overdue and they had run out two days before. While Kambara tended to the girl he returned to his office and reviewed the notes of the tests he had made that morning. It had to be either an unusual female problem or self-destruction, yet the tests were negative, there were no wounds, no bruises, no sign of poison, no symptoms in fact of any common disorder. If she had miscarried, surely she would not be so ill.

It was nearly 11 now, and inside the small room nearby the girl was screaming. "Mrs. Kambara?" he called. She filled the doorway comfortably. "Are you sleeping in tonight?"

"Yes Doctor. But I'll stay up with her."

172

"No, check the other wards and go to bed, because I'm staying on. Would you wake that messenger if he's about and send word to my wife?"

"Yes Sir."

"I'll call you if I need you. And I'd like you to be here in the morning in case we have to—in case there are further complications. Be prepared with an ice-pack."

"I understand, Doctor."

"I would not normally impose on your free time."

"It's all right, Doctor."

When she was gone he moved to his examination table, seated himself and leaned back. A suspicion was taking form; if she didn't yield up the truth he would have to force the matter. He closed his eyes to shut out her cries and resented her for making things difficult. How many more generations would it take out here? How long would he have to sense Europeans, even the sympathetic ones, shrugging over backward Africa?

There was that Fatmata creature, for instance; he caught a glimpse of her as he paced. She was understandable. There was no need to apologize for her. Born in poverty, probably illiterate, possibly abused, horribly fecund, a prey to any man who promised to be nice to her and to any *juju* "doctor" and folk superstition, Fatmata represented an Africa that had to change.

Fatmata was tired of the noise. The girl wouldn't stop her screaming—the pain-devil had her—and all the women were gossiping about it. Since her baby wasn't coming yet anyway, she got up to go home; her neighbor could deliver her again. The women here seemed too noisy and unfriendly. They might poison her.

"Go away, damn Pain-Devil," she called, seeing the devil in the window. The other women glanced at her, then resumed their gossiping. She wanted no more of them. Rising awkwardly from her bed she tied her lappa around her waist, gathered together her bundle, and was about to leave when the nurse-woman entered the maternity ward.

"Ellie, what is the matter with that girl?" called several voices.

"Oh that girl," she exclaimed. "She's got herself into trouble and she won't say how."

"Eh! What will you do?"

"The auntie is coming in the morning. Then we shall see."

"Ohhhh!" the women responded, with many nods.

"Now, where are you going?" The nurse-woman placed herself in front of Fatmata.

"I'm going home," she said in a loud voice.

"But you can't do that."

"There is too much noise here. I can't sleep."

"You lie down there. Your baby is ready."

"Get away Devil," she said, looking over the woman's shoulder. "I've seen you take children."

The nurse-woman shook her head. "Your baby may come tonight."

"I know," Fatmata replied. "I've had eleven babies. I know when it will come."

"Don't be sure. After eleven they arrive quickly."

"Get out of the way, Tearer of Women's Stomachs," she called. "I am going."

"You foolish woman, it's dark outside."

"I have my matches." No harm could befall a pregnant woman who carried matches in her hand—not even the Pain-Devil she saw in the window would touch her.

"That girl will soon be quiet. You must lie down."

Fatmata tied a knot in her bundle and put it on her head. "Perhaps I will come back tomorrow. Don't look at me, Blood-drinker!"

"Think of your baby, you heartless woman."

But Fatmata walked past her, out the door and into the dark. "Think of your baby." What did that woman know? She was no Bundu priestess. The Baby-Killer was after her, and the Tearer of Women's Stomachs. They had hurt her and taken eleven babies from her.

"Dung heaps, don't come near me." She walked a distance along the river, matches displayed in her hand, aware devils were watching but afraid of her. She laughed: They might get her baby but not her. They could take it, as they had all the rest, for she would be glad to rid herself of the trouble it caused in her stomach.

"Filthy excrement, take it. " Nine had walked but she had known the Pain-Devil and the Baby-Killer would

175

get them and so was never surprised. She waved the devils out of the way, balancing her bundle with her other hand, as she turned away from the river. Until this time she had met no one, but now a man was striding toward her. Although she struck a match to be safe, she could already see that it was only the small white man, who knew no *juju*. By the time he passed her she had forgotten him and was looking across the glare from the crossroads light ahead, where she had spotted the Pain-Devil waiting for her, his open mouth revealing his long sharp teeth.

Turner came to Darbah's room twice during the night. After 5 a.m., when he made his second visit, he stayed at her side, for her condition seemed to be deteriorating. It was possible—unless he came up with a diagnosis and early treatment—that this was her last day. A sense of futility came over him: his training, his time, his care counted for nothing in the face of her peasant-like stubbornness. But he continued to work about her, feeling her pulse, listening with his stethoscope, checking the temperature of her feet and then pondering the apparently meaningless findings. Finally the girl woke and whimpered.

"I am here," he said in Mende. He thought she might feel more secure in her own tongue, even though he spoke it uncertainly. "Do you understand me?"

"Yes Doctor."

"You are a Catholic?"

"Yes," she whispered.

"Shall I call the Father?"

She whimpered.

"It's time. Surely you know how sick you are."

"All right," she said, giving way to a sob.

"I'll send for him." But the sky was scarcely blue, an early hour even for the self-important priests, and there was also the chance that Darbah would debate with herself. He left her long enough to freshen his face; when he returned he was perspiring, convinced her resistance would break down. She was saying her "Hail Mary"; as he waited for her to finish he saw that the sponge in the sink was wet and guessed that she had managed to wash away her vaginal discharge again.

"Hail Mary full of Grace, Blessed art Thou among women and blessed is the fruit of Thy womb Jesus. Hail Mary—" she broke off and looked at him.

"There is still a chance to help you," he said in English, "if you will tell me what you've done to yourself."

"It's—just—the fever."

"Tell me," he persisted: "I'm going to examine you again, and keep examining you until I find it. Even if you die, I will know what you've done, (because, he thought to himself but did not say aloud, I will not confess that I couldn't make the right diagnosis), "so why don't you save me the time and trouble?"

She refused to answer. He knew with something approaching conviction what he would find—something truly deep-bush African—but he hesitated over forcing an examination she might resist, and decided he should first send for McCartney. He walked out to the registration desk looking for the day-nurse, but she was going to be late again; the hour hand on the wall-clock had already touched seven. Fortunately, Kambara appeared, on her way out.

"Where is the messenger?" he said. "We must send for Father McCartney. The girl should have last rites."

She pursed her lips. "She doesn't improve, Doctor?"

"No."

"You know, I've sent for the auntie. She's outside."

Turner straightened. "That's good, that's very good. Bring her in, please—look, here comes Massaquoi. Send her personally for the Father and don't let her argue with you. She's late for work."

He leaned against the door of his office, his eyes aching dully, his legs threatening to buckle. Kambara met Massaquoi at the door and sent her off to the Mission compound. In a moment she was back, pulling an alert older woman behind her.

"This is the auntie," she said. "I've told her how the situation is."

"Very well. Now tell her that unless she can find out what has happened, Juliana will pass."

The auntie, protected from the morning air by a green wool sweater, accepted the responsibility stoically. She might have been any age from forty to seventy. Her unwrinkled face was set and stubborn.

"Is she free—by all possible means?" Kambara asked.

Turner yawned. "Oh yes." He watched the duty nurse, on her bicycle, disappear over the bridge. "*Ah say*, yes," he said, lapsing. "Yes, of course."

They walked to Juliana's room. He checked to be sure she was awake, then drew the other two in. Darbah was frightened by the sight of the auntie but dissembled quickly. The older woman went directly to work on her, once the customary greetings were dispatched, while Turner and Kambara stood aside. "Some devil has tricked you," he understood her to say, though her own term was cruder. "There is no use in lying."

"No no," Darbah whimpered.

"Stop it." The woman proceeded irresistibly, her voice taking on a threatening tone. Turner reluctantly admired her brutality. "What did you do?" she demanded. Standing over the girl she drew back her hand.

"Nothing, nothing, nothing."

The hand exploded against Darbah's face and she cried out. Turner went to the window and pulled the curtains. Again there was a slap, and a cry. It's not London, it's not even Freetown, and we have a life to save. He went to close the door, for the auntie was shouting over the girl's screams. It was difficult for him to look at Darbah's face, contorted as it was in pain, and fear of either death or shame. The calloused hand struck out again and her sob sank in misery. He was ready to stop the assault when Darbah said, "Yes, for my job," choking: "They mustn't know."

The auntie looked at him. He wondered if it was the Canadian.

"Find out how," he said, via Kambara. "I have to know exactly what I'm dealing with."

She shook the girl by her shoulder. He turned away from Darbah, impatient and dejected, sensing that the fulfillment he had expected as a doctor might elude him. If with thousands of people to treat he had to devote two days exclusively to one girl, to beat the truth out of her and then possibly to see her die anyway, what was he accomplishing? He wondered if his anger was unfair; was he too Western, had he lost touch with his people? Yet a reasonably well-educated girl who wouldn't tell a doctor the source of her illness?

A few shakes of her shoulder, another slap, and several shouts brought the story, interspersed with sobs, from Darbah's lips. Turner had trouble understanding and looked for clarification to Kambara. It was as he suspected. He hadn't treated anything like it but he knew what was happening inside her, and what needed doing.

"Who gave it to you?" the auntie demanded. He spoke to restrain her but his voice was overwhelmed by that of McCartney, who burst in saying, "Michael, for the love of God, what are you doing?"

The Father himself had scarcely slept. The previous evening Ellie had denied both him and Sister Catherine entrance to Juliana's room on the excuse that the girl was too sick, but later as he sat brooding over his beer Manny had seen his light and stopped in. He reported hearing, a few minutes before, moans he thought were Juliana's and seeing figures moving in her room. The two of them drank together for a time in his small apartment on the mission's ground floor. He appreciated the concern the Canadian was showing for his protege; Manny was rarely so solicitous. What he was still implying about Juliana couldn't be true, but clearly, he had never intended to affront. He was an independent sort, and clinging stubbornly to youth, but compassionate beneath the standoffishness. He wished Manny were a Catholic but as far as their friendship was concerned, it didn't matter.

Their conversation was fitful, and later he lay awake, rolling in his narrow bed. He rose as usual at 6:30 and told Father Clark of his concern over breakfast. Taciturn as ever, Clark merely nodded. McCartney left the table, unlocked his bicycle, walked past his flowers without a glance, and started for the hospital; within a block he saw Esther riding in his direction.

"Esther, would Dr. Turner be at the hospital now?"

"Yes," Esther said laconically. "They said you should go there immediately."

He felt his throat contract. "Is it Juliana? Is it really so desperate?"

The nurse shrugged. "They just said you should go."

He sensed the worst; and wheeling around, he returned to the mission to fetch a container of holy oil. He easily overtook the nurse as she drifted along on her own bicycle and was soon at the hospital. He was surprised to hear Juliana's scream, the more so because in his memory he heard the slap that preceded it. He tumbled off his bicycle and pushed it up to her window. He could hear through the curtains a harsh female voice demanding an answer and Juliana sobbing unintelligibly. Michael spoke next and the strange woman made another demand, clearly manhandling Juliana. Face flushing, McCartney threw his bicycle to the ground and ran into the hospital, bringing himself only partially under control by the time he reached the sickroom. Turner was startled but said evenly, "Good morning, Father."

"Faith, Michael, would you be beating a helpless girl?" Sure enough, Juliana was sobbing and an old woman was hovering sternly over her.

"We are trying to help her."

"What," he said, "by killing her?"

Turner looked at his hands. "Father, you know by now that we sometimes have to do things our own way."

"But a girl ready for Extreme Unction?" He moderated his tone. "A bit late, isn't it?"

"She's told us what's wrong. I may be able to save her."

The hint of evasiveness made McCartney uncomfortable. "I see. But I should administer the rites anyway, is that it?"

"Yes."

"Very well. Then I'd like this woman"—he switched briefly to Mende—"Selina Koroma, aren't you? Yes, I've seen you about—I want her out of the room. And you and Ellie too, if you don't mind."

"Of course. But be quick, Father." Michael drew the two women out with him.

McCartney turned to Juliana, who lay inert except for her sobs. "Now, child," he said in a shaky voice. "Don't be afraid. It's time to put your house in order, you know—confess your sins before God. Can you hear me?"

"Yes, Father."

"Don't be afraid now." He wiped the corner of his eye.

After bringing her breath under control, Juliana confessed to missing mass often and to being disrespectful once to Sister Catherine and finally, to what he had feared all along, the absence of that immaculacy that would become her. Intermediary for God though he had to be, McCartney felt his own unworthiness. His words of comfort pained him. Manny was right; yet he'd been so sure. But what could a man have done in a natural act to injure her so badly?

He pulled out his holy oil, moistened his fingers and dabbed the sign of the cross on her eyes as he prayed for her soul. He moved his fingers to her ears; he moved them again to her nose, feeling annoyance because Ellie Kambara was gossiping loudly outside the door. He touched Juliana's mouth and she stopped all moaning and whimpering.

Almost an angel, he thought. Imploring God to have mercy on her, he anointed her hands. Ellie was still talking in Mende and he began to understand her by dint of her repetitions and even to listen to her. He had finished his rites and said a last prayer when her words fell into place. Juliana too had heard; seeing his sudden rigidity she shrieked. He moved like an angry spirit into the corridor and stepped between the two nurses.

"What were you saying about a child? I heard you, you know."

"I'm sorry, Father."

"Was it that?"

"I didn't realize you understood."

"If you don't mind, I wish you wouldn't evade me questions."

Michael came their way with a gurney full of equipment; looking toward him, McCartney saw the throng of patients who were staring at them. "Esther," said Michael, "why are you chattering when there are all these patients to be registered? Thank you for your help, Mrs. Kambara. Put this equipment in her room and then you can leave." The directness of his commands startled McCartney. Michael came up to him quickly. "What is the trouble, Father?"

"Michael, I want the truth. Did that girl do--" he couldn't go on.

"You know very well I can't breach her confidence, any more than you can." He looked down the empty corridor behind McCartney, rubbing the bristles of his beard.

"But she didn't do anything so terrible?"

Finally Michael looked into his eyes and said, "Have mercy on her, Father."

"What! I give mercy?" he shouted. "There's no mercy for that young woman." Sweating and breathless, he turned and made his way through the crowd without a word to anyone. The open air soothed him, but when he had stationed his bicycle in the mission portico, he felt shame for having let Juliana hear him, and burst into tears.

Erb noticed that the Father had not come to school. He disliked his own malaise and went ahead with his classes. When McCartney failed to appear after lunch, he approached Father Clark and asked after him. Clark was a slight, dark man, as black in his cassock as McCartney was red. His duties around the district left him little time to spend at the school, but one didn't get to know him well in any case, for he was reticent and usually noncommittal.

"Have you seen Father McCartney?"

"Yes."

"Is he at the mission?"

"That's right. He's very busy right now."

Erb scowled. "Well," he said, "how is Juliana?"

"I've no idea, you know. Should I be keeping track of murderers, now?" Clark moved off abruptly, seemingly perturbed at having said so much.

Erb found his palms perspiring. He wiped his hands on his shorts, pulled out his handkerchief and dried his upper lip, aware that Clark's Religious Knowledge class in the room beside his had rested their dark eyes on his face. Haltingly he moved into his own eager class of first-formers. They watched him expectantly, but his thoughts left Juliana only to touch the priest at the mission. He gave them a chapter of their history text to read and without another word walked out to his bicycle to begin the descent into town. Below him the river seemed fuller and faster; the rainy season was coming, and there were dark clouds to the East.

He resisted the temptation to go to the hospital and instead cycled directly to the mission, letting the perspiration trickle unheeded into his shirt, barely conscious of the bulging muscles protruding from his sleeves, or of the racing form on display in the pump of his sinewy legs. To his relief, McCartney made him welcome.

"Manny lad," he said, "come in, come in. We'll have a beer."

"Maybe; that is, if you have time."

The Father moved to the refrigerator in the adjacent dining area, negligently brushing a book off a side table as he passed. Although he and Father Clark shared two servants, McCartney kept his apartment as unkempt as Clark's was neat: Cushions flopped half out of the wooden seats, the bookcase was a jumble, and each of the white curtains seemed to be stained with ink, insects, or grease.

But it appealed to Erb more than Clark's quarters, to which he had only rarely been invited; they had the bare, lifeless look of a Quebec monastery. It oppressed him to think men lived that way, and without women.

McCartney gave himself time to set the bottles and glasses in front of them before speaking again. "Well Manny," he said, watching the beer run into his glass. "It's not something I can discuss, but you saw things that I didn't, about-—"

He cleared his throat. "I don't want to talk about it either. How is she?"

"Ah, it's a terrible thing, Manny, a terrible thing."

"She's gone—?"

The Father seemed unable yet to look him in the eye. "I don't know. It was better she were. You know Manny, the trouble with making Christians of the people is that the ones you trust the most are the ones who let you down hardest of all. Take Michael Turner, a Creole man no less. There he was, supervising a beating of that girl when I found him."

Erb clenched his fists.

"Yes, it's true. That's how they found out what she'd done. Well, Michael's all right—a bit of a stuffed shirt if anything—and perhaps he hadn't much choice. But I'd've been happier, God forgive me but it's true, if she'd just passed on before I'd arrived." He drank his beer a moment as he began to unwind, looking away from Erb's scowl. "Manny, that girl," he said, "—I'm hinting at things that can't be disclosed, but, but, if I hadn't overheard Ellie Kambara's corridor gossip I'd still not know."

"What an ungodly thing she must have done to herself."

The Father smoothed his hair with a big red hand. "Yes, Mike may save her life, but he can't save her soul."

"I didn't mean—" he stopped, but McCartney understood and turned his full gaze onto Erb's face.

"Ah Lad, you have to see it through Catholic eyes," he said. "She's ruined everything for herself."

"Does she know this?"

"If she hadn't understood the faith after all our years of training her, she probably won't understand now. But I'm afraid she knows what the Church has to say about her." He finished his beer. "Can you stay for another beer, and maybe a change of the subject."

"All right." Erb was thinking, Why am I sitting here?

The Father returned from his fridge and they sat quietly over their drinks. "Don't get me wrong, Manny," he said. "Don't get the idea I don't feel personally for Juliana; I do, I do."

Erb was spared an answer by the appearance of Father Clark, or of Clark's head, which floated along above the compound wall. Suddenly McCartney became his paternal self, winking and chuckling. "Look at the Father," he said. "He's too sober, you know. He looks like he's bitten into a green mango, doesn't he? But he's quiet and lets me do the talking."

Erb could not sit still for an encounter with Clark. Mumbling an apology, he rose and slipped by both priests, clambered onto his bike and sped to the hospital, his heart pounding. Most women in this world were Feles; he couldn't care about them. But here was the ultimate feminine, and he was suffused with indignation at the sight of Turner, who had emerged from the isolation ward, stethoscope around his neck, and was heading for the main entrance.

Pushing his bike against a tree he intercepted the physician. "Doctor," he demanded, "how is Juliana Darbah?" He rose slightly on the balls of his feet, looking up.

The other man spoke slowly. "There is some hope."

"That's a wonder." He blocked Turner's path, but noticed the man's exhaustion and stepped back. "You can save her?"

"I can't be that sure. Much depends on her own will to live, and I'm afraid your headmaster has made my task more difficult."

"Father McCartney?" He took another step back. "Well, he thought very highly of her, you see."

"All the more reason for him to be charitable—or at least, silent."

"Damn," said Erb. He disliked this cameraderie; he had enjoyed feeling sorry for Turner's pretty young wife.

Turner yawned. "You must excuse my bluntness. I admit too that my own people perplex me at times; Juliana Darbah is one of them."

Erb's thoughts went to Esther Massaquoi, who had come to and left his flat with a face devoid of interest; to Fele, and to crazy Fatmata, who just then shambled in front of them to the entrance.

"What about her?" he said, pointing.

"Fatmata? Well, you see, she's learned to come here for her delivery. That's progress."

"Do you think this one will live?"

"Excuse me?"

"She's had about ten and they've all died. She thinks that devils kill them."

"Be careful of your Western--" Turner stopped and asked, "Would you see Miss Darbah? I was just going home but I'd like to take you in."

Erb caught his breath. "Yeah, I would. Why?"

"Because a life means something to you." To Erb's surprise, he broke into Krio. "*Ah say, mon, make you no go see 'un?*" He caught himself. "I'm tired; sorry. Please speak with her. If she sees that you care, perhaps she'll care herself."

Erb thought he might have to hold Turner upright, for the man was swaying as though near collapse. "All right. She does mean something."

"She does?" It was Turner's turn to look puzzled.

190

They walked into the hospital wordlessly. Erb rebuked himself: I'm almost 37. Why can't I keep my mouth shut? He changed the subject.

"Tell me, if you can," he said, as they moved along the corridor, "what could she have done that would be all that dangerous?"

"Ah, women." Turner shook his head, glancing at him. "As usual, I've had no luck in keeping confidences. And you're leaving anyway, am I correct?"

"In three weeks."

"I've occasionally wondered whatever brought you here--?"

"Well . . . ." Before Turner could press him, he added, "and I've wondered why you would come to such a backwater with an elegant young wife."

Turner smiled, and after a pause, said, "Intelligent men must go on quests, it appears."

Yes, that's what it is, Erb thought.

They reached Juliana's door. Turner drew him past.

"Since it's common knowledge by now," he said, "you may as well get it from me." He spoke softly, not bothering to look at Erb's face. "Of course it will seem shocking to you, and primitive and stupid—all those loaded words. In any case she was successful, but there are complications."

Erb replied, "I see," but didn't. "Quinine?"

Turner nudged him. "Go on in," he said. "I'll wait for you, but don't be long." He seated himself on a hard chair in the corridor.

Erb felt nauseous. "Are you sure she'd want to see me?"

"No, but it can't hurt."

He turned, hesitated, and entered, with an aversion that increased at the sight of Juliana's haggard face. She was asleep . . . .

He moved to her side and looked at the still-beautiful features. What could he say if she woke: It's me, Juliana, come to explain the quest? Don't you know I almost love you? Don't die Juliana, because I've never held you against me? I'll cancel my trip, I'll stay. Never mind the woman in Utrecht; you've made me forget her?

Gazing on the wonderful figure distinctly outlined by her damp gown, he envisioned maggots swarming around her curves. She made him sick. And what was that smell? Could his dream beauty smell like that, like death? He clapped a hand over his mouth and nose.

Walking out, he decided he would have talked with her had she been awake—about something or other. Perhaps he would come back some time, to say good-bye.

He feared Turner would insist she be awakened, but the doctor himself was asleep and had to be roused. Turner had missed the supposed conversation and was too tired to ask about it. They exchanged nods as the doctor rubbed his eyes.

"Thank you," Turner said. "And now I must go home to my elegant wife. I owe her a bit more of my attention."

"I should go too," Erb replied mechanically.

"Yes, go, Mr. Erb. As soon as possible."

25349748R00117

Made in the USA
Columbia, SC
07 September 2018